GODDESSES

1

HEAVEN SENT

CLEA HANTMAN

AVON BOOKS
An Imprint of HarperCollinsPublishers

For information address
HarperCollins Children's Books, a division of
HarperCollins Publishers, 1350 Avenue of the Americas,
New York, NY 10019.

 Produced by 17th Street Productions,
an Alloy, Inc. company
151 West 26th Street, New York, NY 10001

Library of Congress Catalog Card Number: 2001117949
ISBN 0-06-440875-2

First Avon edition, 2002

Visit us on the World Wide Web!
www.harperteen.com

For Goddesses everywhere
(and that means you)

ACKNOWLEDGMENTS

Without the fabulous Jodi Anderson, this book would simply not exist. She rocks hard and I thank her from the bottom of my heart and my tippy toes.

And a most special thanks to the one and only Miss Keva Marie who helped shape these characters, listened lots, and is an all-around true-true friend.

PROLOGUE

Our story picks up somewhere in the middle. Middle of what? you may ask. The middle of mishap, mischance, and misfortune. The middle of muck. The middle of time-altering, life-changing events that will forever transform the lives of three well-meaning but misguided teenage heroines. . . .

ONE

Oh, poop. I'd surely done it this time.

Daddy sounded mad. Not just Medusa mad but heaven and hell mad. Don't get me wrong; I rather enjoy it when Daddy's a little ticked off. And that's not to say that I enjoy seeing him unhappy. It's just that when he does get a teeny bit mad, well, things get a little more exciting. When Daddy gets mad, the opera unfolds.

But this time it was different.

Era, Polly, and I had just woken up. We'd been summoned as we were, which meant we were wearing only our chiffon nighties. We hadn't even had time to change into our velvet day dresses. The large room where we now knelt before our father was cavernous, cold, and damp, and goose bumps crawled up and down my legs. *Why does Daddy keep the throne room like this, anyway?* I wondered. *All cold and scary and dark?* He didn't even have any chairs. Chairs would have been nice. It's not easy to keep yourself poised perfectly on bended knee so early in the morning.

I looked over at my two sisters and reflected that my hair couldn't possibly look as bad. Era's dangling blond curls were so flattened that they resembled the straw from a stanky old mortal mattress. And although Polly had tried to pull her own long, straight hair back into a ponytail, it was smushed against the sides of her face as if a big ol' vat of the purest Greek olive oil had been poured squarely over her head. They both looked about as icky as I felt.

The three of us had to strain to hear Daddy and Hera argue, even though they weren't but five feet away from us, sitting on their high thrones. They were talking in these loud but echoey and unintelligible hushes, making it almost impossible to tell what they were planning for us three. The problem three.

They hadn't even acknowledged our presence or said good morning or, better yet, apologized for waking us so abruptly. Daddy just continued to talk his nonsense, to *her*. "Well, Hera, I don't know, dear— Tharniasfgh is neeeernddgh and quite bleak. Don't you think raitnghh on two mojld be far treeiergh?"

"I think he said, 'Tartarus is merry with a nice creek. Don't you think that taking on ghouls would be eerier?'" Era whispered, her eyes widening in fear. Era is not the brightest of my sisters.

"I do *not*!" yelled my stepmom extraordinaire, Hera the Evil. And then her tones went back to muffled. "I want them flone, blanirershed, out of cly bears, trerevere!"

"Uh-oh, wait, I think she said, 'I want them done, varnished, and with new hairdos forever,'" mistranslated Era again. "She's sending us to the Beautorium forever! How lovely!"

For the first time Polly took her eyes off Daddy and Hera and snapped her head toward Era, glowering. "Era, don't be such a fool—this is serious. They are not sending us to get our hair done or our nails polished or our legs waxed. They are discussing our demise. Our demise, dear sister. You've both really done it this time."

"Us!" I yelled so loud, my dad and Hera stopped their bickering for a moment to look our way. I lowered my head and continued a bit more quietly. "You had just as much to do with this fiasco as we did. In fact, if I recall, this was your very own idea. I mean, most of it was. I mean, well, I didn't come up with it all on my own. I didn't even *know* about the bag and goat hair and the—"

"Oh, don't you, even," Polly interrupted. But that

was all she said. She pursed up her lips and yanked at her ponytail, then looked straight ahead, her nose tilted slightly in the air. I opened my mouth to say more about the whole "incident," the thing that got us here, but promptly shut it. There was no use arguing with Polly.

We knelt there in our own silence, listening to our father appeal to Hera, Polly looking angry as Hades at me, and Era looking, well, half asleep and half afraid.

"But sweetie, these are my girls," Daddy pleaded more loudly than before.

Witchy-witch Hera just sat above us on her gilded, jeweled throne with her hands crossed, not letting my father catch her eyes, which were now burrowing a small hole in my skull. Or at least that's what it felt like. She had the evil stare of a black vulture at midnight.

I just smiled a stubborn smile at her.

Daddy continued to beg. "But honey, snookums, be reasonable. Yes, the girls have been utterly wretched, but . . ."

Well, I wouldn't have said we were "wretched." I liked to think of our behavior as "delightfully disobedient." 'Course, for once, I knew better than to say that out loud.

". . . but please have some mercy on them for me." Daddy was actually truly whining now. I'd never seen him so, so, so . . . weak.

My father is Zeus. Yeah, *the* Zeus. Ruler of the heavens, supreme master of the Olympians, god of the weather, black clouds, lightning bolts, blah, blah, blah. He's a pretty good guy, although the man is so busy wreaking vengeance and overseeing all of Olympus that he hardly has time to be a real dad. He used to be a *great* dad—always taking me and my sisters down to earth to see the sea nymphs and play with the mortal children. But now he's kind of, well, old. And he's married to Hera, who we've had to put up with ever since my mother,* bless her soul, passed on, leaving my sisters and me behind. The nine of us, collectively, are known around town as the Muses.**

And right now the three of us were in huge trouble. Era was chewing on her bottom lip, obviously worried now that Polly had set her straight about the whole punishment thing. "What is going to happen to us? Hera wouldn't really send us to Tartarus, would she? They don't *really* have nice creeks there, do they?" Her voice was now trembling with fear, and dusky roses of excitement were standing out on her cheeks, making her look even more beautiful than usual—messy hair and all.

"No, they really don't, Era," said Polly, rolling her

---

* Mnemosyne, my mom, our mom, was one of the most beautiful goddesses there ever was. You know how most of us gods are immortal? Well, Mom didn't have it so lucky. I miss her more than anything.

** I have eight sisters total, so there are nine of us. We're goddesses of inspiration, goddesses of the arts, and a real kick at parties.

eyes. "And I wouldn't put anything past Hera. You know, last week I watched her catch a fly in her palm and then she held it up by its little tiny wing and dropped it in her mouth. Just like that. She's the meanest woman I know, and trust me, I have seen a lot of evil in my life. She's so angry with us, my guess is we'll be lucky if she just lets us wait on her hand and foot for the next two hundred years."

"Oh, that's a fate worse than death, don't you think?" I said. Oops, a little too loud.

"I think death would become you, Thalia, dear," said my demonic, sinister stepmom. I turned toward her just in time to see a cruel sneer cross her lips, and the goose bumps crept back onto my flesh. Which was really annoying—I hate it when Hera gets to me. I looked at my father and couldn't help wondering—*How can he not see her inherent evil now?*

But he just whimpered, "Now, dear . . ."

Oh, this was bad!

Hera continued to glare at me.

"Thalia!" hissed Polly. "You just don't know when to quit, do you? Things are bad enough—you don't need to make them worse. It's Tartarus for sure. Oh, my, I will miss the others and the wood nymphs and the talking fountains and Pegasus; oh, Tartarus will surely be it. . . ." And Polly, my dear, always composed sister, began to cry quietly. Her light blue eyes (she has the fairest eyes of us all) just turned instantly wet and vivid bloodred. And let me tell you, red and light blue seriously clash.

Two seconds later Era's bottom lip began to tremble. I had to admit that seeing Polly—the strong one, the practical one—cry was pretty disheartening. It made me want to cry a little bit, too. Not that I would ever let Hera see *that*.

But this really was heartbreaking. The idea of us three scrubbing floors in Tartarus, deep down below the heavens and sky and earth, in the fiery belly of hate, far from everyone we love, was enough to send chills down *anyone's* spine.

You see, Tartarus is this little slice of Hell, actually part of Hades. It's where mortals go when they have offended us gods so severely that we punish them with death. The worst mortals end up there, and it's governed by my three least-favorite girls: Meg, Alek, and Tizzie, otherwise known as (whisper, please) the Furies. If they hear us use that name, they'll go berserk. They prefer to be referred to as "the Blessed Ones."

Those three girls have tormented my sisters and me our whole lives. It seems they live to make our lives miserable. And they often succeed.* The thought of being on their turf, stuck in Tartarus at

---

* See, in the Olympus hierarchy, the Furies are in a class all by themselves. Even my father, while not exactly afraid of them, steers clear of them. They have this all-knowing sense about them, but nobody really knows how much they actually *do* know.

their mercy, was excruciating. No, horrifyingly, hysterically hellacious. My head started to spin at that thought; my eyes started to ache, throb even; the hairs on the back of my neck stood on end. I felt overheated and out of breath.

Both my sisters continued to sniffle, looking desperate and tired. And contrary to what they may sometimes think, I hate, hate, *hate* to see my sisters upset. A vision of Hera falling off her throne and breaking a leg suddenly popped into my head. It wouldn't stop our punishment, but how could we be in any more trouble than we already were? I began to twinkle my nose. But before I even got to the part where Hera would lose her balance, Polly reached across Era and clutched my nose, nearly knocking me over.

"What in Athena's name are you doing?" Polly demanded in a loud and angry whisper. But she didn't wait for the answer; she just continued, "Are you insane? Do not even *think* of using your powers now, not here, no! This is Daddy and Hera, for gods' sake!"

"Fine." I snorted. I shook free from Polly's grip and threw her an angry look. But she was right. I hadn't been thinking. Even if Hera was already planning the worst punishment imaginable for us, I was sure she could somehow find a way to come up with one that was worse.

Era, meanwhile, seemed oblivious. She was thinking aloud of what punishments she could tolerate.
"Perhaps Hera would take a suggestion," she whispered. "I think I could stand it if they took Pegasus
away from us—for a whole month I could, I think."

Polly's patience with me was already gone, and
now her patience with Era's simplicity was truly
wearing thin. "That's a paltry offering, Era, and you
know it. Our punishment is going to be worse than
not having our favorite pet around for a few weeks'
time. You two are insufferable. Need I remind you
that Hera has a will unlike any other?"

The sound of my father clearing his throat silenced
us. Era grabbed my hand and squeezed it, while Polly
regained her stony composure and stared straight
ahead. Daddy spoke. "Girls, you have disobeyed me,
disgraced Hera, had fun at our expense, and acted
like little beastlings."

"Era." Era started to tremble when Father spoke
her name. "My beautiful daughter, while it is clear
these plans were not of your devising, you have once
again gone along with the crowd, forsaking what is
right and just instead of standing on your own two
feet and making your own decisions. You were
swayed too easily yet again. You must grow up. You
must realize that you are a young woman now and
your actions have consequences."

I was pretty impressed. Daddy may be oblivious

sometimes, but he seemed to have Era pinned down pretty well.

Daddy continued. "Polly, my good daughter." Polly nodded dutifully. "What in heavens possessed you to take part in this matter? Well, I think I know. You seek to help others, but at what expense? You need to learn that there is a time and a place for helping. And perhaps even more important, you need to focus on your own life rather than trying to fix everyone else's. This constant meddling in other people's affairs must be supplanted by your own ambitions and desires. While I know you think your heart is in the right place, it is not. For your actions have had dire consequences. Why, look at your step-mother. Look at her!"

Did I forget to mention that Hera looked slightly green at the moment? I couldn't help smiling at that.

"And you, Thalia, do you mock me?"

"No, Father," I said, wiping the smile off my face. Daddy sighed.

"My precious Thalia, how could you do this to me? This is, without a doubt, your most severe stunt yet. You have wrecked lives, you have played with the Fates, you have inflicted damage on those who love you, and why? Because you think it serves you best. Because *you* wanted it so. While making your plans, did you ever spare a thought for anyone besides yourself? No! Don't speak—we all know the answer. You, my dear daughter, need to learn the very opposite lesson from your sister Polly— you must learn to be more selfless. You must learn to let concern for others temper your strong-headedness and selfish desires."

Whoa, that was pretty harsh. But maybe true. A little. Maybe.

Daddy sucked in his breath, then let it out in a deep, reluctant grumble. The noise echoed in the chamber and, I dare say, the whole kingdom probably heard. His voiced reverberated as he spoke these eleven words:

"I have no choice but to banish you three to earth."

Era shivered.

Polly shook.

I . . . I got a little excited.

"Athens, Greece, specifically," Daddy added. "It is the mortal year 423 B.C. there."

"But for how long, Father?" asked Era, her voice barely audible.

"I cannot answer that. Only *you* can answer that."

"Well, then, I will come home . . . tomorrow!" said Era. Stupidly, I might add.

"Oh no, dear, I don't think so," said Hera with a gurgle and a chort, a cackle and a snort.

My father then spoke. "Please, Era, take a step

forward." Era stood and walked to the foot of my father's throne.

"The time will arrive when you may come home.
It is not written in the stars or in any tome.
It is up to you to do what is right.
You may feel swayed by others,
but this you must fight.
Only when this lesson is learned
To Olympus you may return."

He paused and then added, "You may now step back."

Era looked more than a bit confused as she turned and walked back toward us.

"Polly, please take a step forward.

"The time will arrive when you may come home.
It is not written in the stars or in any tome.
It is up to you to live for yourself
And put your meddling ways up on the shelf.
Only when this lesson is learned
To Olympus you may return.

"You may now step back."

I knew what was coming next. I stepped forward.

"Thalia?"

"Yes, Father," I said, trying to keep the excitement

out of my voice. But all I could think about at that moment was earth. Hallelujah! Peasants and satyrs, black seas and Crusades. I always wanted to ride a dragon!

"The time will arrive when you may come home.
It is not written in the stars or in any tome.
It is up to you to put others before you
And not take for granted the friends
who adore you.
Only when this lesson is learned
To Olympus you may return.

"You may now step back."

Hera began to speak, her voice as deep and loud and evil as ever. "One more thing. You cannot use your powers. Not an ounce of your powers." And then she laughed. Oh, she laughed a hideously wretched laugh. She stopped only to add, "And absolutely no one must learn that you are goddesses on earth, or there will be hell to pay, if you know what I mean."

My dad had to speak extra loudly to be heard above her insane, out-of-control laughter. "Please, girls, be careful to heed these laws. Otherwise"— and he looked sideways at my stepmom from hell—"I cannot be held responsible for what will happen."

It's not that bad, I thought. *So we can't use our*

powers. It could be worse. Earth is exciting and new and filled with adventures—I'm sure of it. It'll be great. But then I had another, terrible thought.

"The Furies are gonna have a field day with this one," I said to no one in particular. And no one heard me because at that very moment a light flashed so brightly, it blinded us three and we were

falling

fast and furious

plummeting

into

a

pit

of

pure

darkness!

Two

The journey downward could have been more exciting. Sure, it was scary, with quick turns and vertical drops, but frankly, I was just too excited about arriving on earth and exploring the altars in Sparta and hitting this perfumery in Pompeii that's run by an old gypsy woman to be all that scared. After the first hour or two I got really bored, so as we rushed through the darkness I started making a mental list of all the things I wanted to do on earth. We couldn't speak at all to one another. The force with which we were careening just made it impossible. But both my sisters were in view the whole journey. The thing of it was, the trip really did seem way too long. A whole day's worth of hours just wasted. If I'd had time to expect anything, I would have expected a quick ride that took my breath away. The only thing that did *that* was the hard landing, which not only took my breath but part of my chiffon nightie, too.

After we'd hit the ground, we all just lay there for a minute, stunned. The ground was hard underneath us.

"He didn't even let us grab our clothes." I turned toward Era's voice—she was under a tree, slowly sitting up and rubbing her head.

"Or sneak Pegasus into a bag," said Polly, who was still lying flat out on the dirt.

"Hey, but we have each other," I said a little sarcastically. They both just glared at me. But then I saw Polly crack a smile. Albeit a very, very small one.

With a jolt I realized that we were actually on earth. I think Polly and Era realized it at the same time, for suddenly they started looking around us, their eyes wide with curiosity.

It was dark out, but we could see.

What we saw, we did not know.

All around us nothing looked familiar.

By the light of the moon we could see many small buildings, each one neat and tidy and strange looking. A sort of street ran along the grass where we now sat, and it appeared to be hard and wide. Every street I'd ever seen had been made of dirt. *That* was a little weird.

Era was the first to stand up. She circled a little

bit and stopped in front of a structure of some sort. "This is one odd building, huh, Polly? This must be a part of Greece we've never seen. Not even in picture books."

Polly just stood there, stunned. I knew something was wrong by the look on her pale, moon-shaped face. And not only that; I knew it in my bones. Everything just seemed a little . . . *off*.

"Look, there is a message," Polly said, walking toward the door of the structure. She grabbed a crusty, yellowed paper scroll off the door and shook it. It rolled out, longer than Polly's glorious hair, longer than my longest gown. Down it fell, hitting the ground and rolling halfway down the walk.

"Oh, there is too much there to read," Era said absently, watching some small animal hop off into the woods. "What is that pretty little creature?" Era promptly chased after the animal.

Polly shot an annoyed glance in Era's direction. "This is just great—I'm stuck on earth with my laziest sister and my silliest sister. Such luck."

I guessed that I was the silly one. But that's not such a bad -*est* to be given. I could think of worse . . . stupid*est*, boring*est*, scaredy*est*. I looked over Polly's shoulder. Really, the letter on it wasn't all that long— certainly not long enough to warrant such a long scroll. It was probably just a way of making the letter look bigger and more important than it really was. The gods are pretty melodramatic about stuff like that.

Polly read from the scroll: *"Hear ye, hear ye.'* Oh, it's from Hermes.* It says, *'Welcome, girls. This is your new home. Your father, the great and powerful Zeus, was not exactly up to snuff, um, today. He has accidentally sent you three girls to Athens . . . Georgia.'"*

"Georgia! Where is that? In the Balkans? Near Crete? Where?" Era hollered, panting as she walked back from chasing critters. She had all sorts of twigs and leaves stuck in her long, blond curls.

"I don't know," I said. And I was good at geography.

"It says here it's in the United States. There's a map. Let me read on: *'There has been another slight mishap. Zeus has propelled you, quite accidentally, into the future. Look around: This, dear girls, is Athens, Georgia, 2002.'"*

Polly's face went white.

"Whoa," was all I could say. Daddy's powers were definitely shot. Spent. Done.

"How could he, where could he, why, how?" mumbled Era. "Huh?"

Polly sat down on the stairs that led up to the door, dropping the scroll into her lap. "Okay," she said. "That is perfectly fine. We can handle this. So it's not quite the earth we know. So we're in the future and there's no way to tell what kind of monsters there are

---

* Hermes is basically the "delivery" god. He's okay when he's not delivering wretched, horrible news.

here, or how things work, or whether people are cannibals now. That's okay. It can't . . . be . . . all that . . ." Then my sister started to sob. "Oh, Father. As if this wasn't bad enough already!"

"Now, maybe this isn't so bad," I wondered aloud, sitting down next to Polly and rubbing her back. "I mean, we don't know what the future is like. Maybe it's all leprechauns and roses. Maybe it's an adventure every day. Maybe it's space age." *Space age* has been one of my favorite phrases ever since I heard it from a soothsayer on Olympus.

"Your inconceivable enthusiasm is starting to really wear me down, Thalia," Polly spat out, wiping at her eyes with the hem of her nightie. "Can you put a lid on the Aurora* act? This is treacherous, abominable, and all your fault."

"Excuse me," I said, pulling my hand away from her. "Let's not get in the blame game, okay? I do recall your being present before, during, and after the, um, disaster. I do remember your suggesting the spell in the first place; I seem to recall—"

"Please, stop! My head hurts," Era cut in, her voice trembling. "Please stop being mean to each other. Polly, why don't you just keep reading Hermes's letter, *please*?" Era looked at Polly and me with big, sweet, doleful eyes.

Even though she's just a little younger than me and only a year younger than Polly, it's hard to keep

---

* She is, in essence, the cheerleader of the goddess world.

from treating Era like the baby of the family. For some reason, it's just impossible to see her unhappy. It's just that, I dunno, she's so innocent and sweet and loving, and she has the ability to make me feel guilty like no one else.

"Yes, okay, all right," Polly said, clearing her throat. *"This structure of reasonable size and fashion is to be your home while you reside in Athens.'"*

"Georgia!" I called out, but no one thought it all that funny. Polly read on.

"'Inside you will find comfortable bedrooms, styled to the modern tastes of the time. There is a kitchen. In case you girls do not know what that is, I shall tell you. It is where you will cook things.'"

"Cook things? Cook things! I will not cook a *thing*. That is not the concern of a goddess," stated Era. Polly ignored her and read on.

"'Hera has disallowed you any ladies-in-waiting and servants. I'm afraid to tell you that you will have to provide food for yourselves. As well as do the washing, cleaning, shopping, and dressing.'" Era's face scrunched up in disbelief. *"'But don't fear. Many of these tasks have been simplified since ancient times. There is something called electricity that will enable you to wash dishes and clothes using a machine and create bright light and warmth without using a fire. You'll find switches and knobs all over the house that will let you control these various devices.'"*

"Hey, why don't we go inside?" I suggested eagerly. "We can finish reading the letter in there." I nodded toward the door. I knew I should be concentrating on Hermes's words, but I just couldn't wait to see our house and all the cool stuff in there.

Polly sent me the don't-be-so-optimistic glare. Still, we all went inside.

Inside. Inside our new home. It wasn't so bad. There was this furlike stuff on the ground. Almost like grass but not as cool to the touch. And the walls were a marvelous blue color, more the shade of Era's eyes, a deep and hazy grayish blue. Fluffy seats curved around a black box that looked like a shiny ebony rock from deep in the ocean, only it was almost perfectly square.

Polly sat down by the fireplace. I knew what *that* was. Although I had no knowledge of how to actually build a fire. Era sat in one of the big chairs. Neither of my sisters even looked around. It was like, if they didn't look and see any of this, maybe it would cease to exist. Polly continued to read, and I forced myself to sit down at the kitchen table to listen. *"'Please, girls, follow Hera's rules—do not let anyone know you are goddesses, and please, do not use your powers.'"*

Polly took a break from reading this wretched news to point a wretched finger. "Well, we all know Thalia will not be following that rule, don't we?"

"What is that supposed to mean, Polly?"

"If you can't get what you want, you simply use your powers with no thought or care for anyone else."

"That is not fair!" I exclaimed. "Are you having a memory lapse, dear sister? Because you seem to forget that if *you* hadn't used your powers back in Olympus, we wouldn't be here now. It took all three of us to get us here!"

"Oh, my head!" cried Era, rather dramatically, I might add. Polly continued reading.

"*There is one more rule that Hera did not heretofore mention. And it is extremely important. As you are the human equivalent of teenagers, you must now go to high school every day. If you fail to do so, Zeus will be forced to reconsider your punishment, as the whole point of your life on earth will be to work hard at improving yourselves. Here is a map telling you how to get to school.*'"

"Whoa, what does that mean—reconsider our punishment? And when did this become, like, work?" I asked. It had never occurred to me we'd have to go to a school, like mortals. We were Muses, goddesses—what did *we* possibly need to learn? And besides, weren't only boys supposed to go to school?

I looked over at Polly. She had a curious expression on her face. At first I didn't know what it meant. But it looked a little to me like delight. She had turned a pink punch color, and she had a twinkle in her eye.

Even Era looked a tiny bit more hopeful. "So we'll get to continue learning dance and song like before?"

"I think mortal school is different from that, Era," Polly said slowly. "I think you learn all sorts of things, like poetry and philosophy and science." The corners of her mouth turned up into a tiny smile as she said this. "At least, that is the way it was in Greece."

Era slumped farther into her chair and let out a breath. "Oh, great," she murmured.

"Yeah, great," I repeated, thinking of how horrible it would be to be stuck at school all day when I could be out exploring the world.

Polly shot Era a glaring look, turned to me, sent piercing arrows of hatred toward my heart (or at least it felt like that), and then read on:

"'*Zeus, unbeknownst to Hera, asked me to unearth a few of modern life's ins and outs for you, his beloved daughters. So I have conducted some research by watching some fine TV (that's that black box in front of the chairs. It's magical!) and have compiled it into a top-ten list (they're very popular here).*

10. You must get milk.

9. If you get in an accident, call 1-800-THELAW2. Use the phone. It's that hard thing with numbers and the curly wire. It sometimes makes a ringing noise, and when it does, you should pick it up.

8. *If you have large thighs, it is important to hide them with vertical stripes.*

7. *See yourself in Feria.*

6. *Earth, too, has eternity, but apparently here, anybody can have it, not just gods, and supposedly it smells quite nice.*

5. *If you can't find it at the mall stores (where you buy things), then surely you can find it on-line (not sure where that store is, but maybe you can ask someone).*

4. *I suggest giving a woman named Cindy Crawford a call. She seems to know a lot about everything.*

3. *If you can't find her, then try calling someone who goes by the name Oprah. And besides, it's fun to say her name: Oh-prah! Oh-prah!*

2. *The true test of a perfect bra is how it makes you feel.*

1. *For everything else, there's MasterCard.*

"Oh, this is rich. Hermes* as an arbiter of all things cool? Puh-lease!" I said.

"*The last item is important. I have procured you a MasterCard. This is how one acquires goods here (they don't barter with animals and jewels). You simply show this plastic card and voilà! People will give you the things you need. You'll also notice a stack of green slips of paper under the kitchen sink (the basin with knobs that squirt out water). This is cash money—another way of paying for goods. Always make sure to have some on hand.*

"*Now, I must finish this directive, for Hera has*

---

* This from a god who wears tacky gold wings on his shoes?

summoned me so that I may announce to the kingdom, heavens and earth, that you dear girls have been turned into horrifically disfigured monsteresses and been tossed into the future. This, I am afraid, is how she gets her kicks. Good luck. Please, girls, I beg of you to follow the rules Hera has proclaimed. I do so hope to see you three again, eventually, one day. Although with Thalia there, I must admit that I'm highly doubtful. With great love, Hermes.'"

I scowled at Hermes's last comment. It didn't sound like he had tons of faith in us. Or me, in particular.

Era curled into a ball in her big, oversized chair, hugging her knees. The look on her face was something one notch shy of pure, unadulterated fright. The sort little children get when they can't find their parents but before they have a chance to let out a deep and painful wail. I waited for her wail. But it didn't come.

Polly just looked exhausted. Pained and exhausted. None of us said anything for probably ten whole minutes. We just sat there in silence.

Then the wail. Era let out this cry, this loud, quivering cry: "I doooonn't want to go to schooooooooll! It's work—it's not fun; I want to go to the Beautorium and I want to eat pretty little sandwiches with handsome young men and I want to dance and sing and play with my *good* sisters. I hate you. I hate you. I hate you . . . Thalia!"

"Look, it's not going to do you any good to blame me or Polly. . . ."

"Oh, I don't blame Polly. I blame you! We wouldn't be in this mess if you had just succumbed to how you really feel about Apollo. He loved you, Thalia, with all his soul, and now look at us. What will become of us?"

Yep, that hurt. "Oh, okay, fine. It's not going to do you any good to blame *me*." I paused for dramatic effect before launching into my soon-to-be incredibly inspirational speech. "C'mon, girls, this can be like a game. We can ride dragons and play with the fairies. So we'll have to go to *school* in between." Polly's mouth hardened into a straight, angry line. "It won't be long before we get to return home. Look how selfless I am acting right now, giving you this great pep talk. We're halfway there—I'll prove that I can put others before myself in no time. C'mon, let's enjoy the adventure."

"I don't want to go on any adventures, Thalia," Polly said quietly. "Maybe some of these things sound interesting and new and different. But I simply don't care. I want my old life back. My beautiful serene life. The one where I woke up to a choir of blackbirds every morning, singing just for me. Then Lady Josephine would bring me a large bowl of ambrosia. Who's going to bring me a large bowl of ambrosia here?"

But she didn't wait for an answer. Not that I was going to offer to give her one. Sure, maybe they had gotten themselves into this for my sake, but they had offered to help, right?

Polly continued. "And then she would lay out one of my twenty finest silk gowns, unless of course it was Tuesday, in which case she would lay out one of my velveteen pantsuits so I could take Pegasus for a ride through the heavens. After I dressed, she would bring me my jeweled crown because I couldn't go out without my jeweled crown. When she placed it on my head each morning, she would say, 'Oh, goddess, high priestess of the heavens, woman of the world, I bow in your presence, for you are a supreme being worthy of any woman's idolatry and any man's love.'"

"Yeah, but didn't all that bowing and supreme-being stuff make you uncomfortable?" I asked, but Polly kept going as if I hadn't said a thing.

"And then she would escort me down those long, gilded stairs, how I miss those stairs, and then I would meet up with Clio and Calliope and we would play the harp together for hours. . . ."

"And . . . then," continued Era, "I would meet up with you after my fabulous morning at the Beautorium, and we would all dance through the gardens on our tippiest toes, twirling and singing and twirling some more. And Pegasus would lie beside us, watching our every move. And occasionally we would see some boy, a god or even one of the servants, stealing glances at us from behind the large honeysuckle tree."

"Boys?" I said. "It all goes back to boys, doesn't it? Don't you think of anything else?"

But that just set them off. Both of them. Their idle dreaming turned into pointed rage, pointed squarely at me.

I couldn't understand either one of them—they were both screaming and yelling at me at the same time. I heard words like *beastly* and *selfish* and *scolly wog* (I don't know what that means, either). And then each of them stood up and stormed away, stomping through two separate doors, neither of which we had yet explored, and slamming them simultaneously, hard.

I just sat there at the table, in the kitchen, where we were to cook things. *Cook things.* Goddesses don't cook things. Maybe this wasn't such a grand adventure after all. I hated the idea of cooking and cleaning—those weren't *real* adventures. And what good were adventures anyhow if I had no partners in crime, for both my sisters were truly miserable and blamed me and only me. And school? What would that really hold for us? Era was right—it sounded like, well, work. The word *work* sends chills down my spine.

I laid my head down on the cold table. It was filled with sad thoughts of work and cleaning and errands. Thinking of all those things made me grouchy. And sleepy. I hadn't realized how tired I was until just that moment.

Exhaustion came over me like a wave. My eyelids started to flutter. Better to get some rest, I thought, and think about everything in the morning. But just before I fell asleep, a single and horrifying thought popped into my head: *Could this, in fact, be the dreaded Tartarus . . . in disguise?*

THREE

That whole night I dreamed about Apollo. About the look of disappointment and hurt on his face the last time I saw him. And about all the stuff that I did to make him feel that way.

So what happened? What got us into this mess? And why, if Apollo loved me so much, did I hurt him like that?

Well, I was hoping to tell this whole story and just kind of gloss over that whole thing because it's not something I'm proud of. But now I'm thinking that it's the most important part of all. And I guess I have to tell it if any of this is going to make any sense. So I'll shed a little light here. And maybe tell a bit more later.

Anyway, here goes . . .

Apollo* was just standing in Daddy's chamber when I got there. Which was surprising because, number one, I hadn't expected him back that night, and number two,

---

* Apollo is the seriously cool, seriously fun god of music.

Apollo and Daddy don't usually hang out all that much.

I was excited to see my best friend. He had been gone two whole weeks, and I'd been dying to tell him about how I'd swapped Hera's wig with this one I made out of rat hair, which suited her much better. And tons of other stuff that only he could appreciate.

But then I couldn't help but wonder what business Apollo could have with Daddy. And why had I been summoned? I figured I was in trouble, but for what this time? I'd already been punished for the wig incident.

But then, I was always being called into Daddy's throne room for my little indiscretions. You know, embarrassing an upper-echelon god, making my wicked stepmom cry, little things like that. Getting into trouble was a typical part of my day.

It's just that I was always getting bored. I wanted to be more than just party entertainment. Back on Olympus, my sisters and I are sort of a "freebie." If you have a party and you have some stature and standing in the Titan community, then we have to sing and dance for you and your guests.

It's law.

It's scripture.

It's boring.

I mean, occasionally it's fine.

For Daddy, well, okay.

But for every Tom, Dick, and Harry Olympian it simply isn't fair.

And so I guess I just acted out sometimes. And Apollo was usually my partner in crime. He was devilish. He was adventurous. He was loads of fun. 'Course, he wasn't looking so fun at the moment. Probably an act, I thought, for Daddy's sake. To cover up his guilt. Oh, what in heavens had he done? I was obviously being implicated as an accomplice! I just hoped I was going to get blamed for something good. Something awfully good.

Apollo looked still and stoic and, well, terribly serious.

"You rang?" I asked nonchalantly.

"Thalia, my dear, dear daughter. Your manners, please," said Daddy, nodding toward Apollo.

"What? It's just Apollo—cut me some slack," I replied. "Hello, Apollo."

Daddy rolled his eyes at me. "Thalia, you know, you are really a favorite of mine. You have a mind all your own, and you are never afraid to express it. I admire that in a goddess. Just don't push your luck," he said, and with that he winked at me.

Apollo just stood there, stiff as a board.

"Slay any dragons while you were away?" I asked him.

"No," he said, almost under his breath, his eyes diverted from mine.

"What's wrong? Did that witch over in Athens finally find out about what you did to her cat? Did she put a hex on you? You seem so out of—"

Daddy cut me short. "Thalia, please. Now, we have

some news. Some fabulous, grandiose news that I am just certain is going to thrill you to no end."

"Well, can you please just get to it, then?" I asked eagerly. I longed to be thrilled.

With another roll of his eyes Daddy said, "I am a very happy man today." He glanced back and forth between me and Apollo. "Thalia, Apollo is here because he has asked for your hand in marriage. And I have agreed that this will be a fruitful and prosperous union."

At that moment the world just seemed to freeze. I looked back and forth between my father and Apollo, confused.

"Oh, sure," I said, venturing a nervous smile toward Apollo. "This is one of your jokes, right? Well, you're a riot. How did you ever get Daddy to go along?"

Apollo opened his mouth to say something, but Daddy cut him off. "This is not a joke," he said to me sternly.

I stood there, wide-eyed and stunned. "But this is ridiculous," I choked out with a nervous giggle. "Apollo, you know I don't want to get married. Why are you doing this? What . . ." A lump the size of a melon was starting to form in my throat, and I couldn't catch my breath.

"Silence!" my father roared. "Of course you want to marry Apollo, Thalia," he explained. "Stop this nonsense. You two have much in common, and you obviously love to be with each other—I see it in your eyes, in the gardens, at the festivals."

"What? You're kidding, right? Arranged marriages

are so 100 B.C.! You can't be serious. C'mon, Apollo? Daddy?" Fear and shock were quickly turning to anger. I could feel the blood throbbing in my head.

"Enough, Thalia," said Daddy.

"This isn't even fathomable! What do you know of my feelings? Have you ever asked? Have you ever asked me, Apollo?" I cried, turning to my friend and trying to keep my hands from shaking.

But Apollo didn't look at me. He didn't answer me. His face was unmoved outside of the slight flush of his cheeks and the quick dart of his eyes away, far away from me.

"Apollo? Apollo!" I cried again.

"You have no say in this matter, dear daughter. The engagement commences now. You will be married in a fortnight. End of discussion."

"It most certainly is not the end. I will not get married. Shall I count for you both the innumerable reasons? One, I am far too young. Two, while I am very fond of you, Apollo, and enjoy hunting with you and lunching with you and shopping with you and fly-ing with you, I do not think I love you like a wife. I don't think so. No, I do not. Three, I am too young. Oh, I said that one already. I want to be a huntress and go on battles and never marry and—"

"Silence. Thalia, the time has come for you to grow up."

And I could tell Daddy meant it. He didn't say another word for a whole long minute. I looked at Apollo again, and he stood there stiff as a board, looking stunned, his mouth pressed into a thin, straight line. I think he was almost shaking like me, but he was fighting it something fierce. I felt a twinge of guilt—I didn't want to hurt him. But get real. I was far too young for this.

"I don't think I need to marry to become a grown-up," I spat. "I don't think I have to listen to my father's ludicrous ideas or stand here and feel sorry for a man whom I do not love."

Apollo winced.

"Enough," Daddy roared. "How dare you talk to me like that? This marriage will take place whether you like it or not."

"You cannot make me."

"You obviously have not been paying attention. I am Zeus. The great and powerful Zeus. I think this marriage is the best thing for you, and Hera thinks you need to grow up, and therefore you will marry. Now, leave my chamber at once. You must begin preparations. Leave."

Apollo did not say a word. His breaths were low and shallow. His face hard. It broke my heart to see him as such, it really did, but sympathy is not a reason to get married. Still, what choice did I have?

I knelt at my father's feet. "Please," I whispered. "Please, Father."

He just bellowed that awful word again. "Leave."

And so with that I left.

FOUR

That first night on earth I dreamed about this stuff all night. And the very first thing I said to my sisters the next morning was a heartfelt "sorry." I really meant it. It wasn't just because of the nightmares I'd had. I'd had a minor epiphany sometime before dawn. My sisters were here because they'd supported me through the whole Apollo situation, even at a hefty cost to themselves. So I decided I had better start feeling some remorse. And besides, if we weren't getting along, who was I going to talk into making me some food?

Era rushed over and hugged me so tight, my back made a monstrously large cracking noise. Which, to my surprise, felt outrageously good. It was stiff from falling asleep at the table.

Era is a sucker for an apology. She might have

gone to sleep mad, but she can't stay that way, especially when she hears the *s* word. And Polly, well, she
simply doesn't like conflict of any sort.

"I suppose we have no other choice but to just
barrel ahead and do this. Together," said Polly with
her trademark sweet smile. "It's the only way we will
ever live up to Daddy's challenges, and besides, I do
love you, Thalia, even when you're a selfish little girl
with only adventure on the brain."

Hmpf.

"Well, I'm hungry," said Era. And I was, too. We
took a good look around the kitchen. We opened the
cupboards and doors but couldn't find anything that
resembled food. It was obvious: Hera was out to
starve us. This had probably been her plan all along.

"No handmaidens, no cooks—how does one
survive?" cried Era, her perfectly heart-shaped lips
turned down in a pout.

"You know, maybe they have food at school,"
Polly offered.

"Do you think they really could have food there?"
Era asked suspiciously.

"I think so."

I didn't really buy it—I figured this was just
Polly's way of getting us to go to school. Still, I was
willing to try, for food. And we had to go, anyway.

"Only one problem," I said. "While I don't know
much about this modern-day-earth thing, I have a

feeling that chiffon nighties with big holes are not proper school attire."

"Doesn't your room have clothes, Thalia?" asked Era.

"My room?"

"Yes, your room. Mine has some clothes, and although they aren't velvet and silk, they aren't awful," said Era.

"I haven't been to my room. I have a room?" I wondered aloud.

"Surely it's that one," said Polly as she pointed to an unexplored closed door.

I opened it to find no clothes. Just a strange, shiny white basin with a silver handle—it looked like a fancy, modern version of the toilets I'd seen when I'd visited earth in the past. There was also another basin big enough for someone to lie in—a bath, I guessed. But who had baths and toilets inside? That wasn't very civilized.

"I don't want this room," I called out.

"Well, you can't have mine," said Era. "I need it. The bed is almost as soft as my bed at home. I need my beauty sleep."

"There has got to be another room. Let's have a look around," said Polly. But we looked. And there was no other room. Daddy had screwed up again. Urgggh.

"You're just going to have to use that room with the bath, Thalia. Now let's get dressed and get to school," directed Polly.

"Whoa! Wait a second—I'm not taking that room. One of you must share. This is not acceptable, wholly incomprehensible, and—and—and . . ."

But then I thought back to my early-morning epiphany. And the reason we were here. And I shut up. I would take this little room with the tub and the toilet. It was what I deserved. And who knew, maybe when things calmed down a bit, I could trade with Era. This room had one thing Era loved that I bet her room did not have: a big, well-lit, almost glowing mirror. Just like the one in the Beautorium, Era's most favorite place back home.

"Never mind," I said.

"This will be fine," I said.

"I'll take what I deserve," I said.

"Let me just fix my hair in this incredibly gigantic mirror and I will be ready to go," I said. Hey, it couldn't hurt to plant the seed early.

"Well, you'll need to wear some different clothes, Thalia. Come into my room, and we will pick out something," said Polly.

The clothes were wild. Polly had already picked out the most plainest Janest dress of the bunch, which was fine because it meant more of the good stuff for me. I found a skirt the color of a ripe orange and a shirt the shade of a juicy plum, which I thought would look perfect with my dirty-blond bob. But the shoes were the best. They were almost squishy soft,

not like the itchy rope sandals we wore back home.
And they tied up all tight to my foot. And they were
bright turquoise and shimmery silver. I felt like I
could run a thousand miles in these shoes. So what if
I had to sleep in a tub from now on? I had fancy new
shoes. Life was swell.

Era came into Polly's room, her cheeks flushed
and rosy, dressed, well, like a goddess. She'd piled her
hair on top of her head, but some of her long, golden
blond curls wouldn't obey, and they cascaded down
around her shoulders. Her dress was beautiful and fit
her as if it had been sewn straight onto her body.
Trimmed in lace and beads, it was befitting a goddess. The only odd part was that she had chosen
these painful-looking shoes that pitched her foot forward and into a teeny-tiny point. Era is dainty, sure,
but she has massive feet. I couldn't believe she had
gotten them into such achingly small shoes.

"And how are you going to walk in those?" asked
Polly. In case you haven't noticed, she's the practical one.

"They're not as uncomfortable as they look. And
besides, now I tower over even you, Polly."

"Take them off."

"No! You can't tell me what to do. These shoes are
the best thing about this dreaded place. They stay."

"Fine, do as you please, but you will not be using
your powers to get home later when your very own
feet feel like they're going to fall off."

I kept quiet. I was on Era's side on this one. She and I had found something in common on earth. Sure, hers were high and pointy and mine were flat and squishy, but amidst the hunger and awkwardness of our new life, we'd both taken solace in shoes.

Seeing as we were starving and now, hopefully, appropriately dressed, we decided to set off. Polly grabbed the directions to school, and we headed outside. Athens, Georgia, really wasn't much like Athens, Greece. But it was beautiful. The streets were lined with cherry blossom trees (at least I recognized the trees), and a moist, hot wind blew the little white leaves all around us by the thousands. They looked like tiny little enchanted snowflakes.

Polly's eyes smiled. The sights and smells of nature do it for her every time. Sure, there were lots and lots of houses everywhere, but there were dogwoods and azaleas, too. We turned right onto a large, wide street and saw some buildings that sort of resembled the structures back home. They were awash with bright white and had tall, lofty pillars out front. They were nothing like our new house, which was simply a well-lit box with dead ferns out front. Polly would probably fix that, though. She has a green thumb.

"I don't smell any food yet," said Era, who was hobbling along a few steps behind us. Polly told her to be patient.

"Well, so far modern-day earth seems to be completely devoid of leprechauns and dragons. How do you think a girl is supposed to have fun around here?" I asked after a few minutes.

"You don't even know if leprechauns are fun," Polly replied. "And I know for a fact dragons are not. What about these monstrously loud horseless chariots everyone seems to be riding? They look like fun, sort of."

"Yeah," I said, watching one of the chariots race by us. "They look all right. Figures Hera and Daddy didn't provide us with one of those."

A few minutes later we came to a stop in front of a huge building. "Here we are," said Polly. "I wonder what we do now?"

Just then a plump, energetic woman came rushing our way. Her cheeks were all flushed. "You girls must be the new exchange students, the Moose sisters, is it?"

"Actually, it's pronounced 'Muse,'" I said.

"Very well, good, okay, I'm Mrs. Haze, and I'm the assistant vice principal. Welcome to Nova High, home of the Titans. Now, you girls are late, so let's get a move on. Which one of you girls is Polly? You, dear, the tall one, are you the eldest?" But she was looking at Era. It was the shoes.

"No, I'm Era. Is there food here?"

"Ha, aren't you delightful, your host parents sent you off this morning without breakfast? You poor things. Well, just hold on a few hours and you can get lunch in the cafeteria. Now, Polly, your first class is literature with Ms. Oakes in room 3B; that's through these doors, turn left at the nurses' station, go five doors down and turn right out on to the courtyard, then make your first left and third right, and you will find the class in there. Go on, hurry, you're already late."

"But—but we're not together?" Polly stuttered.

"No, dear, of course not. As I'm sure you know, your sisters are freshmen, and you're a sophomore. Now, hurry, go on. Oh, wait, here is the rest of your schedule. You can meet up with your sisters at these steps after school. Now, run."

Polly can't resist doing as she is told. She rushed off to literature, alone.

Mrs. Haze then turned to Era and me. "Now, you two have your first class together. Biology with Mr. Zeitland." Era turned to me and beamed. "Come this way—I will take you there." We followed Mrs. Haze down the hall and passed what we could only assume was the aforementioned cafeteria. The smells of food wafted outside and into the hall. It wasn't ambrosia, but it did smell edible.

"Please, we must stop here and eat," Era begged.

"Sorry, no can do, they aren't finished cooking for another two hours. Gosh, you really are a hungry little thing, aren't you?" She looked at Era sympathetically.

"Okay, let's stop in my office. I've got a candy bar in my desk you can have. It isn't all that nutritious, but it's something to put in your belly."

We stopped in Mrs. Haze's office, and she pulled out a small, shiny brown log with writing on it. Era grabbed it and bit right into it without even offering me any. "Dear girl, you have to take the wrapper off first; where did you three come from, anyway? Don't they have candy bars there?"

"No, ma'am. No candy bars in, um, Europe."

"Hmmm." Mrs. Haze gave us a dubious once-over.

"This is sooooo delicious; it's so sweet," cooed Era as she gobbled the last bite.

I didn't need any, anyway.

Mrs. Haze then took us to our classroom. We walked into dead silence. Every eye in the room was fixated squarely on us. Mrs. Haze whispered something to the teacher, Mr. Zeitland, and then everyone in the room started whispering.

"Class, please welcome Nova High's new exchange students, Era and Thalia Moose. Girls, would you like to tell us something about yourselves, like where you're from, or your hobbies?"

We just stood there, looking at each other. "Um, Europe," I said, taking my cue from Era, which probably wasn't my smoothest move. Everyone laughed.

"Europe, okay, where in Europe?" asked the teacher.

"Uh, Greece," I said.

"May we sit down now?" Era asked. "My feet are killing me."

Everyone laughed again, and Era smiled and curt-sied. She loved having every eye on her. She loved being the center of attention. I didn't really mind it, either.

"Sure, go ahead and take those two empty seats on the right."

My heart started to race, in a good way. Everyone looked so, well, different and exotic and beautiful. Not beautiful like my sisters and some of the other goddesses, but more like incredible paintings or unusual plants. Beautiful because they looked so unique.

All eyes seemed to be watching our every move as we sat down. Era was moving very self-consciously, positioning herself perfectly in the stiff wooden chair, fluttering her eyelashes and thrusting her chin out proudly. I wondered if I looked as nervous and excited as she did.

"Class, please be still," said the teacher. "I need to talk to Mrs. Haze outside for a moment, so just be patient and quiet—I'll be back in a flash."

They left the room, and everyone started to chat. The back row of the classroom was lined with pretty, perky, perfect girls. Three of the girls were huddled together whispering, and for a second my eyes met with one of the three as she slipped a folded piece of paper to the other two. Then they all smiled these Cheshire, mile-wide grins my way. For some reason, the looks in their eyes gave me the chills, and it took a huge effort to smile back with the same kind of smug, fake expression that they were flashing me.

"Wow, look at all the handsome young men." Era giggled.

"Oh, please," I said, shifting uncomfortably in my seat. "Those girls in the back—have you noticed, they're just staring at us?"

"Everyone is staring at us. Everyone," Era crooned happily.

And she was right. At that moment Mr. Zeitland came back into the room, and everyone quieted down.

"Okay, where were we? Yes, so now we were talking about the various species of native American tree frogs. Who can tell me what the common name for the *Phylomedusa bicolor* is?"

"Monkey tree frogs!" I shouted.

The class laughed again. A lot.

"That's right—very good, Thalia. Say, what do we say next time, if you know the answer, you raise your hand. Then I will call on you for the answer. Okay?"

I raised my hand. Mr. Zeitland looked at me funny and said, "Yes, Thalia?"

"Okay," I answered.

"Don't be a smart-ass," he muttered, and then he went on to lecture, dryly I might add, about frog gizzards. I felt a little bit hurt by that comment, but whatever. I didn't see the problem—I'd known the answer, after all. Isn't that what school is all about? Anyway, I could already tell I'd prefer to socialize and people watch than pay attention to frog talk. Maybe this place could be my adventure after all. The kids were all so wild looking. They didn't look anything like my sisters or me. Sure, they had eyes, a nose, a mouth, hair, and all that jazz, but they looked so, so cool. Even the girls in the back looked cool, although they didn't act it—they just whispered through the whole lecture. Sure, the lecture was boring, but that was just plain rude. Something told me these girls took pride in being rude.

"Thalia?"

"What?" I asked. It was Mr. Zeitland. "Do you know the answer to this one?"

"Can you repeat the question?"

"What is the milky white substance that releases from the glands of the giant toad?"

I raised my hand. "Yes, Thalia?" he said dryly.

"Bufotoxin. And it's often poisonous, or at the very least causes irritations in humans," I said.

Mr. Zeitland looked a little stunned. "That is correct."

Bufotoxin is a very popular ingredient in goddess spells. You can wreak all sorts of human havoc with just one giant toad, a winter white peach, and a snippet of Amazon hair.

It felt good to be smart in front of all these people. Although Polly, Era, and I are pretty young compared to most gods, we've still been around for thousands of years in human terms. Long enough to learn some stuff. Okay, a lot of stuff.

A girl with purple hair (purple hair!) looked my way and gave me the kind of smile that simply said, "Cool." Very unlike the kind of smiles the girls in the back row were flashing me now. Their smiles simply said, "Witch." But I decided to just ignore them.

A bell rang, and everyone got up and pushed their way out the door, despite the fact that Mr. Zeitland was still in midsentence. The girl with the purple hair came over to us. "Hey, I'm Claire. Thalia, right?"

"Yeah, nice to meet you. This is my sister Era," I said.

"So, like, what class you got next?" Era and I looked at our schedules that Mrs. Haze had given us before she left. "Geometry," I said.

"Cool," said Claire, "follow me." And we did. As we walked into the hall we saw the three icy back-row girls leaning up against a row of lockers, just staring us down. The tallest one, with dark, curly hair looked at me and said, "Hey, you're really smart." Era smiled, but I just kept silent. "How do you know so much about frogs? Is that what you used to eat in, um, *Europe*?" All the people standing around the lockers started to laugh. Maybe these people weren't so cool after all.

"Yeah. We eat them all the time. I guess it's kinda gross," I said, looking at the beefy guy standing next to her, his arm looped around her shoulders and a slimy grin on his face, "but at least they're not as slimy as *that* guy." My new purple-haired pal Claire giggled, and I grinned at my own witty comeback. I'd had a lot of practice trading insults back home, with girls who were far smarter and craftier than these three. I lifted my chin as Claire, Era, and I strutted away in cool silence. That is, until Era whined, "I want another candy bar!"

FIVE

$\mathcal{E}$ra and I had our morning classes together, but by the afternoon we were separated. Neither of us ran into Polly all day, so when we all met after school on the front steps, I was thrilled to see her. And she seemed genuinely happy to see us.

"I talked with a girl today who told me we can get food from this market that's only two blocks from our house. Let's stop there on the way home," said Polly, her eyes sparkling just a little.

"Well, Claire, our new friend who has purple hair, she says the best food is from this little place called Weaver D's," I sang happily. "And get this—they make it for you. We don't have to cook. We won't starve after all!"

"I like the food here at school," said Era. "Polly, I ate three of those candy bars, two little bags of potato chips, and this long sandwich someone called a hot dog. At first I was horrified, but it's not really a dog," Era added. "Anyway, I'm still hungry."

"Let's just try the market," said Polly.

"Why?" I asked.

"Well" —she paused, wrinkling her freckly nose— "I think we should be learning while we're here. You're the one who wanted adventures, Thalia. Cooking could be an adventure. Why don't we cook tonight and try your Weaver D's place tomorrow? Okay?"

"I guess. Claire says all the cool kids go to Weaver D's. But fine." We walked to the store, Era hobbling barefoot two steps behind us. The shoes had finally gotten to her.

"Hey, guys, wait up," she said, sitting down on a rock and rubbing her feet. "I have to take care of this—my toes are killing me." And with that, she started wriggling her nose.

"Era!" Polly yelled, jumping forward and covering Era's nose. "I told you, no powers! Do you want to get us into more trouble than we're already in?"

"Oh," Era said sheepishly, standing up slowly. "Sorry, I forgot."

We continued walking. "So, Polly, was your day as grand as ours?" I asked.

"It wasn't so bad."

Then all of the feelings I'd felt all day just started

spewing out of me in one huge breath: "Well, I met so many new people, and they were all so exciting. Like Claire, she has purple hair and all sorts of jewelry, but way better than Hera's gaudy stones. She's just very modern and wacky and, well, she tells it like it is and she's so nice. I mean, she shared her lunch with Era and me today and, well, it was delicious. And I know Olympus is home and all, but I think this could really be a fun adventure, and while I know you don't like all that adventure talk, don't you think this could be splendid?"

"It's not exactly supposed to be a vacation. We should be working on our tasks, you know, our punishment . . ." said Polly, all adultlike. "But I don't know—maybe it won't be terrible."

"I love it here!" yelled Era, several feet behind us now. "There are so many new boys here I've never met. My goodness, they are heavenly! I knew all the boys back home already, and frankly, I was tired of them."

"Boys, boys, boys. Do you ever think of anything besides boys?" I snapped. I didn't mean to yell at Era, but boys weren't exactly my favorite subject these days. Boys were the last thing on my mind. Or at least they should have been. *Well, one boy in particular should have been.* Still, I'd been thinking about Apollo all day, especially during my debate class. It was just that he was the best sparring partner I'd ever had. If I said that Neptune had a cool beard, he could go on endlessly, rapturously about how Neptune actually had no beard at all and in fact had never had a beard, much less a cool one. And in the end, I swear, I would've believed anything he said.

Suddenly I noticed that Polly was giggling. That snapped me back into reality—my serious-and-deeply-troubled-by-our-new-life sister was *giggling*. Obviously she'd had a better day than she'd let on. "What's up with you?" I asked, taking a closer look at her.

"Nothing. I just like school, that's all. You know, the books and stuff." The light sprinkling of freckles on her nose stood out against her pale, flawless skin. She looked practically radiant.

"Yeah, I know," I mumbled, but I didn't. I mean, I liked learning, I guess. Really I liked knowing the answers. I liked being smart. And I'm sure Polly did, too. But she seemed happier than the kind of happy one gets over books. You know how book happy is an inner, private happy that makes you feel warm, cozy, and smart? Well, Polly seemed to be carrying around a whole boatload of happy on the outside. *But,* I told myself, *Polly has a mind all her own. Who knows what's going on inside her head?*

Two guys in a fancy red chariot slowed down in front of us to scream: "Era! Era! Meet us at the Varsity!"

"Who was that?" asked Polly, shocked.

"Some boys I met today in Latin. Cute, huh?"

"I couldn't tell," Polly said. "What's the Varsity?"

"It's another one of those places that makes food for you," I said, because I knew. Claire had told me all the hot spots for people watching and good food that you don't have to cook yourself.

"Well, then, let's go there," said Era. In case you haven't guessed, boys and food are Era's two favorite things. "Please, let's go there, please."

"Tomorrow. Today we're trying the market," Polly said sternly.

"You said tomorrow we could go to Weaver D's," I cried.

"Fine, tomorrow Weaver D's, the day after we will go to the Varsity!"

"How come you are dictating what we do?" asked Era.

"Because you, my dear sister, are the youngest, and Thalia, well, Thalia is the most irresponsible of us three and, face it, prone to flights of fancy. Had I taken charge back on Olympus, really taken hold of the reins myself, I dare say we wouldn't be here right now."

"Are you really sure I'm more irresponsible than Era?" I asked, smiling at Era.

"Pretty sure," said Polly.

"Thanks, I guess," said Era.

And for some reason, we all just started laughing.

That silly sister laugh that comes from knowing one another too well.

Outside the store a few minutes later, we watched an older humpbacked woman grab a metal pushcart and wheel it inside, so Polly did the same. "I'll assume you fill this up with food?" she asked, but neither of us answered. Like we knew.

The inside of the market was dizzying. I had never before seen so much *stuff*. Even Daddy's cook's kitchen didn't have one-seventieth this much food. At least I thought it was food. Frankly, outside of the fruits and vegetables, it all looked foreign and inedible to me.

Polly took charge. "Okay, let's start with what we know. Apples, oranges, pears, plums. Oh, there is grapefruit over there. Grab a few of those, Era, would you?"

"Look," I said. "They got carrots. How do you think we cook 'em?"

"I don't know. We will just put them in a pot and cook them. I'm sure it will be delicious. Grab a bunch."

Onward we pushed to an aisle labeled Breakfast. There were boxes and boxes lining the shelves, each one with a different picture on it. Era loved these boxes. She wanted four or five. None of us had any idea how they would taste. But more important, Polly didn't know how to cook them, and I surely didn't. That's when Era marched up to a handsome young man and asked, "Sir, excuse me, how does one cook this?"

"You're kidding, right?" he asked back.

"No, why, is that funny?"

"Is this some sort of high school prank?" he asked her again.

"I don't think so, and why are we talking in questions?" she asked. "I'm not from Georgia, and we don't have these boxes where I am from. Is it hard to cook?"

He laughed. Like out loud and from the gut. "You don't cook it. You pour it in a bowl, you pour some milk over it, and you eat it. Voilà," and with that he turned and pushed his cart in the opposite direction, laughing.

Era was thrilled. "Yippee! No cooking! Let's get lots of these boxes. And then we must find the milk. Hooray, I will not starve! I will eat Fruity O's and Choco-Stars."

Polly wasn't sure we could survive on cereal alone, so we pushed on.

We picked up some hard, frozen boxes in the aisle marked Frozen Food. And we loaded up on colorful cans and more boxes in another aisle, marked Ethnic Foods. All the boxes had pretty pictures on them, and—luckily—what appeared to be directions on how to cook them.

Polly and Era seemed very happy with themselves,

but I wasn't satisfied yet. We'd traveled a really long way to earth—we might as well dine on the best it had to offer. We just needed to find out what that was.

As we turned into the last aisle, I spotted those three very pretty, very snotty back-row girls from bio. They were huddled together, whispering. Didn't they ever do anything else? That uncomfortable feeling came back over me, and I thought about walking away, but then I remembered who I was. I decided to be the bigger gal and to ignore the fact that being near these girls was making my heart beat just a little faster than usual. Maybe we'd just gotten off on the wrong foot. I walked straight up to them and said, "Hello. I'm taking a poll for the, um, the government of Georgia?" Governments did polls, right? "What is your most favorite food?" Hey, maybe I could get some real info from these chicks.

The one with the raven-colored stripes in her hair said, "Anchovies. Aisle six."

The one with the pale porcelain skin said, "Sardines. Aisle six."

And the one with the cold black eyes said, "Pickled pigs' feet. Aisle ten."

None of them said it with much of a smile. I thanked them; they winked at me; I suffered through a shiver down my spine. We started to walk away, but just before we turned the corner, Era pitched forward with a jolt, landing flat on her stomach in the middle of the aisle. Peals of laughter rang out from the girls behind us. I turned to throw a nasty look their way for being so rude, but even though their laughter was still echoing through the aisle, the girls themselves were nowhere to be seen. That's when I noticed that my heart was pounding again, this time louder and faster than before. I let out a deep breath and headed toward my sister.

"It's those shoes," Polly chided Era as she pulled her up off the ground.

"I swear, it wasn't," Era said, dusting off her clothes and looking confused and embarrassed. "One minute I was just walking, and the next minute I simply lost my balance."

"It's called tripping," Polly said dryly. "On your shoes."

After helping Era up and combing the whole store, we had amassed quite a bit of food. I was ready to leave. Polly got in the longest line. "This one is shorter," I said, moving to the one next to it.

"No, it's not," she replied, a little out of breath.

"Clearly it is. C'mon, I wanna get home and play with that microwave thing."

"This line is fine. We're staying," she said emphatically.

"Ohhh, candy bars. I want some of these, okay, Polly?" asked Era.

"Sure, go ahead." Era grabbed like twenty of them and placed them in the cart.

When we finally got up to the front of the line, the mortal who put our food in the bags commented on our choices. "Dude, what's with all the cereal? You girls having a slumber party?" And then he laughed at his joke. I smiled to be polite, but I didn't get why he thought his joke was so funny.

"Whoa, do you girls really eat this stuff? Pickled pigs' feet? Oh, man, that's gross. Look at that. That's so very gross. I am so glad I'm a vegetarian."

"Me too," said Polly, very quietly. She didn't even look up when she said it.

"Hey, you're in my lit class, aren't you, the new girl, right?" he asked. His name was Tim—it said so on his bright red vest.

"Yes, I'm Polly—it's nice to meet you."

"Yeah? Cool," he said.

She smiled. He sort of smiled. This was weird.

"How will you be paying for this, ma'am?" asked the girl standing behind the counter.

"Um, MasterCard?" said Polly.

"Do you gals need help bringing the bags out to the car?" asked Tim.

"No, we don't have a car," I said. Polly shot me the look of death.

"We can manage, but thank you," said Polly.

"Cool. See you in school, eh?" And then he was on to other people's food.

As we walked out of the store, a thought pecked

at my brain. Finally I had to ask her. "Polly, is that guy why you wanted to come to the market?"

"Don't be ridiculous, Thalia—what a ludicrous thought. How dare you insinuate such a thing!"

"I think the lady doth protest too much." I'd learned that in English today. Cool, huh?

"What the heavens does that mean?"

"You sure are making a bigger deal of it than I did. I just asked a simple question. You gave me more than a simple answer."

"These candy bars are so good. You guys wanna try these?" Era mumbled between mouthfuls of her favorite new food.

"No!" we both answered in unison.

Polly went on, "Boys are the last thing that should be on our minds. This shopping excursion has nothing to do with Tim. I just wanted some food, okay?"

Aha, she had noticed his name, too.

As we walked down the street, pushing our metal cart filled with Cocoa Lemmings and Sugar Nutz, pigs' feet and Uncle Sal's Vegetarian Bean Burgers, I could see splotches of color standing out on Polly's fair cheeks. And she kept muttering softly to herself, "We are not here to meet boys, we are not here to meet boys," as if she needed to be reminded.

Six

Boys were the first thing on my mind the day after Daddy announced his ridiculous plan to make me marry Apollo. Well, namely, the stupidity of boys . . .

That morning I jumped out of bed and headed straight to the Beautorium. I needed a steam bath to clear my aching head, and I needed to talk to my sisters—who'd already been asleep when I'd gotten the news the night before. I recounted the story to Polly, Era, and Clio*, fittingly in a roomful of hot air.

Clio immediately put herself in charge of the engagement party. "Oh, it will be fun, Thalia. We haven't had a good party in ages."

"How can you say that? This isn't about a party—this is my life."

"Sorry, it's just that I—I mean, we won't have to

---

* Clio's my bossy sister. Even bossier than Polly.

sing at this party, just dance, with whomever we want. It will be so grand."

"Hello? You're not thinking here." I pleaded with her to see it my way. "This means I am getting married. As in marriage, as in I won't be around here much anymore. Can I get a little help, please?"

"I'm helping," Clio said. "I'm crafting you the best party Olympus has ever seen!" And with that, she left the steam room to go get her nails done.

"Era, Polly, what am I to do?"

"Well, Apollo is really handsome," said Era.

"What? It's just Apollo!" I said.

"Are you going to tell me, Thalia, that you have not noticed his creamy, most perfect skin? Or his piercing dark green eyes that fall soft when you are around? Or his incredibly round and firm behind?" asked Era.

"Stop! What are you saying?"

"I'm saying he's gorgeous, male perfection, smart, sassy, and stunning!" said Era.

I was shocked, completely shocked that this was how my sister saw him. To me, he was the same boy I had played with in the clouds when I was five. The same boy who had eaten mud pies with me, courtesy of the Furies. Okay, so now that I thought about it, he had lost some of his baby fat. Maybe all of it. I wondered why I had never noticed.

"And jeez, besides being extraordinarily handsome, he is so sweet to you," said Era.

"Yeah, well, yes, he is, but that, well, we're friends. I am sweet to him, too."

"Not exactly," said Polly.

"What is that supposed to mean?" I asked.

"It's just, well, you're harsh with him; you tease him and make him do things for you. Thalia, you're a little bossy," Polly said.

"No, I'm not. I mean, that's the way we are. We tease," I explained.

"You still make fun of his lisp. He hasn't had a lisp since you were eight!" Polly cried.

"He doesn't have a lisp? Not since we were eight? Nooo." I surely would've noticed that.

"It's true," said Era. "Apollo, he is fun, really fun. Remember that time that you and he and that Amazon from—"

"Sure, whatever. I mean, I know," I practically yelled. "But I want to have a life of my own. I want to run in the Caledonian boar hunt and go on Crusades. I want to swim with the mermaids and fly with the eagles. I want to go on adventures. I can't do those things if I get married."

"But he's so very kind, and wouldn't he want you to go on adventures, too?" Era asked.

"Doubtful. Once you're married, life as you know it stops. Or so it is in all the books, right, Polly?"

"Well, no, not always," she said.

"In all those books I read . . ." I went on.

"All those books, eh? I can't remember the last time I saw you pick up anything but that gossip scroll Hermes puts out," said Polly.

"Anyway," I continued, ignoring my sister, "it's different after you get married. Look around. Do you know any adventurous couples? Take Daddy and Hera, for instance. Daddy's full of life and excitement, and Hera sits on her throne all day long, just getting her hair done and polishing her jewels. . . ."

"And what's wrong with that?" asked Era.

"Puh-lease! Haven't you been listening?" I moaned.

"You know, Thalia, I bet Apollo is different," said Polly.

"You don't know that," I said. "Apollo—Apollo is stubborn, and he's pretty high up there as far as gods go. Don't you think I'd be expected to be the good little goddess? Stay at home, look pretty, wait patiently for him to come back from fighting monsters and giants and flooding cities and all those sorts of things?"

Era shook her head. "It's just that, well, they're not asking you to marry ol' King Cepheus;* they're asking you to marry Apollo, your best friend. Your very cute, very sexy best friend."

"I know, I know, I know, but boys and marriage are not the magical key to a happy life."

"Right," said Era, as if she didn't believe a word of it.

---

* Icky old Cepheus actually sacrificed his own daughter, Andromeda, to save his kingdom from Poseidon. Yikes.

Polly had just been sitting there quietly, taking it all in.

Still, I think she knew in her heart that I was born to run with wolves and laugh with centaurs and slay dragons. She hadn't ever said as much, but we had an understanding. She, too, believed boys and marriage were not the key.

"You really don't want to marry Apollo, do you? I mean, are you sure as sure can be?" asked Polly.

"Um, yes. Yes, I am," I declared.

"Well, maybe you can run away," suggested Polly.

But before I had a chance to even imagine it, she took her suggestion back. "No, Daddy would find you . . . anywhere."

"Maybe I could marry Apollo in your place," Era said.

"No!" I cried. That was not what I wanted, either.

"It was just a thought. Maybe you do want to marry him after all."

"I do not. But you offering yourself to him is clearly not the answer."

"Hey, I'm just trying to help," said Era.

Hmpf.

"I've got it. You will get sick, really sick and horrid. And Apollo will not want you then," suggested Polly.

"But I don't want to be sick as much as I don't want to marry Apollo."

"Ah, but what if you weren't really sick?" said Polly.

"Okay, where are you going with this?"

She paused, deep in thought, and Era and I both hung on her breath, waiting for her words.

"What if you go and apologize to Daddy and what if you tell him you made a mistake, you will indeed marry Apollo. Then at the grand engagement party you become frighteningly sick with—with—with Scyllia disease! Oh, oh, oh, your head will sprout serpents and you'll sprout extra limbs and you will be covered in the smelliest of sea scum and Apollo simply will not want you then."

"Polly, there is no known cure for Scyllia—even Daddy cannot cure it."

"Exactly!"

"I'm still not following you."

"Me neither," said Era.

"The other day the Furies came to visit Hera. I overheard them talking and, well, Hera was out to punish Pegasus because he has repeatedly gotten into mischief at your orders instead of obeying hers. The Furies had brought Hera this book—it was a book of Hades's secret spells, and they were showing her how she could freeze Pegasus's wings without any of us knowing how or why it happened. I was shocked, and I just hid out of sight, listening in. They became distracted moments later when Hera had to show off her latest jewels Daddy got her, and, well, I—I sort of stole the spell book. I know it's not right, and I was so sick with myself that I didn't tell anyone. But you see, I've been reading it, I couldn't help myself, and you know, it's actually extraordinarily fascinating."

"You shouldn't feel bad—you saved dear Pegasus from frozen wings!" I cried.

"But stealing is not right. I still can't believe I did it. Anyway, I do recall a spell contained in the pages of the book. I believe it went something like this—if three of us put our powers into Hera's charmeuse bag with a snip of the hair of a young goat boy, we three could give you a proxy of the disease that will last but twenty-four hours."

"My smartest little white witch of a sister, you are a savior! It's brilliant!" I declared.

"Wait a second—I dunno. We could get in a heap of trouble for this," said Era fearfully. "Maybe you can just leave me out?"

"But we need you, Era," I all but screamed. "The two of us alone cannot do it—we need a third, plus you are the only one of us who can get close enough to a goat boy to snatch a lock of hair."

"True, true. The goat boys do love me. But I just don't know. If Father finds out, he will be so very angry."

"Please, Era, even Polly's willing, and you know how straight and narrow she is. I mean, she's like our most uptight sister and . . ."

"Hey! Be nice. I came up with this 'brilliant' plan, remember?"

"Right, sorry. So Era, please? For me? I cannot marry, I just cannot."

"Well," Era said, breaking into a proud grin, "I really don't see what the big deal is, but since you seem so adamant and, well, because I love you so very much and, well, since Polly is going along with it and, well, you do need me, don't you?"

"Thank you! You're saving my life, really, Era, you are. Both of you are. You are saving my life."

A sense of relief flooded over me. Maybe there was a way out of this after all. But a nagging question stood out in the back of my mind. Didn't Hera or the Furies notice that their spell book had gone missing? And if so, what were they doing about it?

For some reason, the hairs on the back of my neck stood up at the thought. It made me wish I knew what the Furies were doing right at that very moment, just so I could make sure that, whatever it was, it had nothing to do with me or my sisters. . . .

※ ※ ※

We choose to pick on the Muses of nine,
Not for their behavior, nor their bustlines,
But because of their annoyingly sweet little actions
And their loathsome and trite self-satisfactions.
It goes but against our Furies credo:
Be dark and mysterious complete with bad mojo!

Are these three so foolish that they forgot to check

✱ HEAVEN SENT ✱

Who was listening in on their devious dreck?
Apollo was to be Tizzie's love of her life,
But now he wants Thalia to be his lil' wife?
Well, horrors on her and demons on him,
We'll turn their plan upside down and out on a limb.
Those three can give Thalia the Scyllia disease,
But the very first person she touches will feel dizzy,
And then they too will turn all ugly and smelly,
Their skin will become mutant green mint jelly,
And that person will have Scyllia for good,
Not some twenty-four-hour fake gobbledygook.
And who do you think she shall touch that first time?
Our dear Apollo for sure—we'd bet our fine rhymes!
Apollo will never love anyone evermore,
And on those three Muses we will even the score.

✱　✱　✱

SEVEN

Anyway, back to the life on earth.

We'd been in Athens, Georgia, for a week, and yet we'd had not one opportunity to complete Daddy's challenge. No progress whatsoever. Zilch. Zero.

"I just love these Pop-Tarts—we need to get more, okay?" said Era, sitting on the ground in the middle of the school quad, scarfing down cold Pop-Tarts one after the other.

"I guess. Personally, I don't know how you eat that stuff. And for lunch? It's so sugary sweet. I think you need some more carrots in your diet," replied Polly. "And something green, too." Era rolled her eyes, but she picked a piece of celery off Polly's plate and started gnawing on that—wincing the whole time.

"So, we made it," I said cheerily. "One official school week. How do you feel?"

"I feel good. Although I wish we could eat lunch together every day like this. That part doesn't seem fair," said Era.

On Fridays the whole school had lunch at the same period. Otherwise Era and I were together for the first half of the day, then from there we were all separated. It wasn't that bad—I got to eat with Claire and her friends Pocky and Hammerhead, and they made me laugh.

Era continued. "But, you know, I quite like it here. The scenery is nice. Very nice." At that moment a young football stud, Jimmy J. Johnson, went walking by. I was plenty sure Era wasn't speaking of the plants, which, while attractive enough, weren't nearly as spectacular as back home. No, my bets were on Jimmy J.

Jimmy J. took a seat with my backroom arch-nemeses, the three witches from science. "See those girls?" I said, pointing them out to Polly. "Claire calls them the Backroom Betties because they always sit in the back of the classroom and gossip. They hate me and Era, and for what reason?"

"They especially hate you," Era said matter-of-factly.

"But why do they hate me at all?" I moaned.

"It's simple," Era replied. "You're smart. And gorgeous."

"Really? You think I'm smart? And gorgeous? My beautiful sister, well, aren't you just the sweetest. But those are not reasons to hate someone."

"Thalia, you know better than that. Jealousy is just as alive and well on earth as it was on Olympus."

These were wise words coming from my sister's mouth. Especially that part about me being smart and foxy. Maybe this place was truly having a positive effect on Era. I couldn't say the same thing for my elder sib, though. Polly was sitting with us physically, but her mind was obviously somewhere else.

"Yo, Polly. What's up?" I asked.

Nothing. She said nothing.

"Polly, hello, earth to Polly. What on earth has got you all mystified and tongue-tied?" I asked, making a little rhyme.

"What? Oh, it's nothing. Math. Algebra. That's all."

"You're daydreaming about algebra? You are not related to me," said Era.

My thoughts exactly.

"Um, English. I have a big test in my English literature class," Polly said distractedly.

"Literature is your best subject. What's the matter with you? Are you sick?" I wondered.

"Fine, I'm . . . perfectly fine," she muttered.

I watched her eyes follow this young, black-clad guy with thick, long hair and one of those I'm-trying-to-grow-a-beard-but-I'm-just-too-young faces. He came out of the math building, crossed the quad, and went into the English building. There was a look of pain on his face, like the instrument he had slung on his back (which looked like some kind of wooden, oddly shaped harp or something) was just too heavy for his delicate frame. And something about him looked familiar, but I couldn't place him. In any case, he kind of seemed like a weenie to me. A moderately cute weenie. But then, Claire said half the boys at school were weenies.

Surely my sister was not looking at this guy. No, it was impossible. I didn't even bother to pursue it.

"So, what do you both think I should do about those torturous Backroom Betties? Polly, they taunt us and tease us throughout class, especially me. Mr. Zeitland is simply clueless. They pass notes around making fun of my clothes, and they've begun to start rumors about my past. Oh, this one was rich—on Wednesday the 'note of the day' said, 'We heard Thalia was born of freakish circus stars. Pass it on.' I got it from Claire; she intercepted. I swear, it takes all my willpower to keep from turning them into black-footed frog-lizards."

"Don't worry about it," said Polly absentmindedly.

"But they're making fun of you, too, when they say that. If my parents are freakish circus stars, so are yours."

"What are freakish circus stars?" asked Era.

"Well, I had to ask Claire that, too, and she said they are traveling performers who live out of trailers and juggle balls and wear clownish makeup and train lions and stuff."

"That doesn't sound all that bad to me," said Era.

"Yeah, I know. But Claire made it sound like it was awful, so I assumed it must be. I swear people have started to look at me funny in the halls," I said. If only they knew who our *real* father was.

"You know," I mused. "It's only been a week since we were banished, and I've sort of forgotten Daddy. It's not like he ever spends time with us, anyway, since Hera came along. And he never lets us have any fun."

"Well, on Olympus we got to dance and sing and play twenty-four hours a day. What about that don't you call fun?" said Era. Then she added, "I miss home."

I expected Polly to mimic Era, like my old parrot Wilhemina, but she didn't. She didn't mention home. She looked off, toward the English building, in a daze.

"'Course, home doesn't come with Jimmy J. Look at his fine behind. Even the gods back home don't have rear ends like that." Era's homesickness had lasted all of five seconds.

"Beware, though, after spending ten minutes with those Backroom Betties, Jimmy J. will think you not only have circus freaks for parents, but that you smell of cabbage and don't wash your socks. That would be Tuesday's and Thursday's Thalia-bashing notes. And, well, you are my sister, a geek by association."

"You *don't* wash your socks," said Polly, back from some other universe.

"Nice of you to join us," I said.

"What?"

"Polly, can you pay attention to us for, like, five whole minutes?"

"Oh, right, the world revolves around Thalia; I must pay attention to Thalia. So sorry, Miss Thalia, high priestess of the galaxy."

"Okay, I did not deserve that. What is the matter with you, Polly? Why are you so—so—so on edge?"

"I'm simply not in the mood to chatter on about silly spiteful girls or cute-butted Johnny Jims or cabbage breath," she said defensively.

Well, she was sort of paying attention.

But then *he* walked by. Out of the English building, through the quad, and right by our bench. The long-haired guy with the pained look. He waved coolly at the Backroom Betties, winked at a pretty cheerleader, slapped high five with a random jock or two, and then pitched his chin my sister's way. My *big* sister's way. And Polly's eyes followed him every step of his journey. He nodded at her, smiled a sly sideways smile, and kept walking. My sister never blinked. She watched him, bright-eyed and bushy-tailed. And I swear, right when he passed our bench, she gasped quickly and quietly for air.

Era didn't notice him. She was too busy straining

to hear what the Backroom Betties were saying to Jimmy J. But I saw him. And I saw my sister see him.

It was the same guy, the very same guy from the grocery store.

"You like him," I blurted out.

"What? Who? No," she said, unconvincingly, I might add.

"Yes, you do. Oh my gosh. Polly, you like him."

"Thalia, I'm not here to meet boys. I just want to make Daddy proud and go back home. I do not like him. I don't." This time she said it firmly, but then she smiled a teensy, tiny little smile. My heart clenched.

Why did I feel so protective all of a sudden? It wasn't like me to worry about my big sister. So *what* if Polly had a crush on someone? It might loosen her up a bit. *Besides,* I reasoned, *Polly's smart enough to handle a little romance.* He wasn't *that* bad. He was kinda cute in a scruffy sorta way. If Polly liked Mr. No Shave, I decided, it was her right, and I would help her have him. Then another thought occurred to me. Daddy *had* said I should put others before myself. And he did say that Polly should find a life of her own. Maybe we could slay two dragons with one stone. Maybe we'd be on our way home sooner than we'd thought. And even though I kind of liked it here, I had to admit it wasn't as exciting as I'd hoped. I missed using my powers. I missed Apollo. Not that I thought he would ever talk to me again.

"Well, I gotta get to class. I will meet you two after school right here, okay?" I said. I needed to get started on my new mission ASAP.

"Why are you going to class so soon, Thalia?" asked Era. "We still have ten minutes before the dingdong rings."

"Yeah, I know, but I have some stuff I must do for, uh"—I looked down at the folded sheets of paper lying on the table in front of me—"the school paper. See you girls later," I said, and I dashed.

As I walked away I could hear Era wondering aloud, "Since when is she on the school paper?"

EIGHT

I tried to catch up with the black-clad grocery boy named Tim but lost him in the crowd. *Well, he may not be my dream guy, but he gets points for being fast,* I thought.

After losing him, I looked for Claire but couldn't find her. And so I spent the extra ten minutes just chasing people to no avail. I finally had to give up and go to class. Which, by the way, was exceedingly boring, excessively boring, more boring than I ever thought possible. I doodled and thought about all the ways Tim was probably fabulous. He had to be: My sister, my keep-her-nose-in-books-all-day-long sister, was attracted to him. I daydreamed that he was supersmart and worldly and poetic. I thought about how he and Polly would look walking down the halls of Nova High together. I thought about all the attention they might get as the coolest couple in high school and how I, as her adorable little sister, might reap some popularity benefits.

At the end of class I found Claire and finally got to ask her . . .

"So, who is that guy who's always wearing black, the hairy one?"

"You mean old man Fisher?"

"No, the student, the one with the scruffy face who seems to know everyone?"

"Oh, you mean Tim Rhys? Why do you want to know about him? He's a full-on poseur."

"What's a full-on poseur?"

"Heh, heh, heh. A poseur is someone who pretends to be something he's not. That Tim guy pretends to be some worldly poet and musician, but really he's just a popular jockey, playing each group, attempting to climb the social ladder to complete studdom. But truth be told, he's a fake. Please don't tell me you find him attractive?"

"No, no, not me," I said, fiddling with my notebook dejectedly. This was really not the kind of guy I wanted for my sister. But then, who was I to say who she should be dating? It was all about getting her *own* life, right? I looked up from my notebook to see Claire staring at me curiously. I decided to change the subject.

"So you didn't tell me, what did today's Backroom Betties note say about me?"

"Oh, that. You shouldn't let it get to you—those girls are worse than poseurs. They're downright mean little witches."

"I know, but what did it say?"

"It said, 'Thalia and her sisters are aliens. Pass it on.' But you know no one believes a word they say, right? And the people who do are so clueless, they're not worth your time."

"Uh-huh, right." I paused. "What's an alien?" Claire tilted her head and squinted at me, then she started giggling.

"Oh, Thalia, you are too much. Aliens? You know, little green guys from outer space? You guys don't talk about aliens in Europe?"

"Oh, nah," I replied, a little embarrassed. But it was impossible to feel all that embarrassed about that kind of stuff around Claire. She seemed to think all my little questions and dumb mistakes were funny and kind of cool.

"Well, thanks for being my friend, anyway. Even though I am a dirty, smelly, circus-freak alien."

"You're the nicest dirty, smelly, circus-freak alien I've ever known. See you tomorrow. And stay away from Tim Rhys."

I didn't bother to set Claire straight. I wished I could tell her it was Polly who liked Tim and I agreed he was a poseur, but that it was really important for Polly to find a boy of her own. But telling

Claire why *that* was would mean telling her about Daddy's challenges, and telling her about Daddy would mean . . . well, I just didn't want to get into it.

Ugh. I let out a sigh. The only shot I had at fulfilling those challenges was to help Polly find love. And that didn't seem so appealing now.

Both Polly and Era were already at our meeting spot on the bench outside when I got there. As I approached them, so did another. One Tim Rhys.

"Hi. Polly, right? I'm Tim. I just wanted to tell you how much I enjoyed your poem today in lit class. It was very powerful. You have a true gift."

Polly looked at him, wide-eyed and stunned. She didn't say anything, just smiled.

"Hi, I'm Era. Do you play that thing or what?" Era said, nodding at the instrument Tim had strapped over his back.

"Um, you mean the guitar? Yes, I play some tunes," he said, smiling as if he was trying to look modest but failing miserably. "So, Polly, what do you say we share our Rossetti notes? I'd really love to hear what you have to say about her feminist themes. I have a real postmodern take on her work that you might enjoy hearing. I rather pride myself on being a cultured guy. Yep, I have to admit, I'm a rootin' tootin', red-blooded feminist."

My sister just stood there and nodded.

"Okay, then. How about we talk Monday after

class? Have a great weekend." And he left. Without saying so much as a good-bye to Era or myself. Maybe he *was* as smitten with my sister as she was with him. And why not—she is supersmart and incredibly beautiful. Maybe he wasn't so bad after all. Maybe Claire was wrong.

"What's a feminish?" asked Era.

"I have no idea," said a flushed Polly. Her cheeks were beet red, the color of the most brilliant hibiscus flowers.

"Well, he seemed to be hot for Pol, eh, Thalia?" Era said, poking Polly.

"Wha?" Polly asked, still in a daze.

"He was practically drooling over you," I said, trying to sound enthusiastic.

"No, he wasn't," said Polly, snapping back to her own practical self.

"Yes, he was!" both Era and I screamed.

"No, no, *no*! And besides, I have no interest in him."

"How on earth do you expect us to believe that, Polly? If you're going to lie, you'd better start trying a little harder to conceal your real emotions. You actually trembled when he was talking to you."

"Okay, fine, I think him cute. And smart. And worldly. But that's all."

"That's enough," cooed Era.

"Anyway, he's very popular here. I'm quite sure he

has no interest in me outside of my English notes," said Polly.

"You are being way too modest here," I said truthfully. "But don't worry—leave it up to me, and you shall have your unshaven man."

"*No!* Thalia, no! I beg you, no. I forbid you to interfere."

"You can't forbid me. Forbid me? Forbid me from doing you a favor. Oh, please, Polly."

"I'm serious, Thalia—don't do anything. Anything at all. Don't you remember, you're the one who's always saying that we did not come here to meet boys? Don't start making efforts for love on my part. I'm perfectly happy just as I am, just as things are."

"You're clearly not. You've been mooning around the house since we got here. You've been dazed and confused. You've been . . ."

"Lovesick," said Era.

"Take it from someone who knows," I said, putting my hand on Era's elbow. "You are lovesick."

"Stop! I mean it. You are to do nothing. Leave him be." Polly sighed. "Let's just get home—I'd like to watch that TV thing some more."

"All weekend!" enthused Era.

I, too, had become totally addicted to TV during the short time we'd been on earth. The talk shows, the reruns, the WB. I loved the drama, the clothes, the way people talked. Not to mention it helped me pick up all the modern words and phrases.

"TV works for me," I chimed in.

Just then a shiny jet-black chariot, which I now knew was called a car, slowed down alongside us. Inside were my least-favorite girls: You guessed it, the Backroom Betties. The three evilest ones from science. They just stared us down as they drove on by. I felt that familiar tingly feeling again, like something bad could happen at any moment, and I had no idea what it was or how to stop it. The feeling went away, though, as the car pulled out of sight.

"Yep, those girls are evil," said Era.

I couldn't have agreed more. In fact, something about them reminded me of home.

✳ ✳ ✳

Yes, we three Furies have a brand-new name,
The Backroom Betties, we are one and the same.
With some crafty time travel, we arrived first
To ensure that the Muses' bubble is burst,
Which will be easy, we cannot tell a lie,
Since the eldest has fallen for that unshaven guy,
And, of course, poor Polly will not make such a match
For this is our plan, which we have just hatched:
Thalia's efforts will all amount to a sham,
And Polly will be betrayed by her man.
She'll be so ashamed, she'll give up on school

✳ GODDESSES ✳

And break one of Hera's strictest earth rules,
For we know something that the Muses do not
Since Hera confided to us three her plot
That if the Muses give up on going to class
A new punishment will soon come to pass,
The streets of earth they will no longer roam,
Tartarus will become their permanent home.
Now let us get back to our craft, our own little coup,
We need to make more trouble so there is a book two!

NINE

"*Your father, he said you wanted to see me,*" Apollo practically whispered. I had been waiting for him in the Prism Gardens, and he had snuck up on me from behind. I could feel his breath on my neck. The little hairs at my nape tingled. I was most certain it was a draft, because I had never noticed that happening around him before. Surely I had been this close to Apollo in the past.

I turned around quickly and found myself just inches from his face. His face, which at that moment in time looked nothing like the Apollo I knew. His jaw was clenched tight, his gaze cast down his perfectly straight nose at me solemnly.

"Your father said you had something to tell me," he said stiffly.

"Yes, I have something to say."

I tried to manufacture a smile. This was far harder than I thought. And not just because I didn't want to get married. I hated lying to Apollo. He was my best friend. And right now he looked so serious, so foreign to me.

"Thalia, now first, listen to what I have to say, please," he said, his eyes softening into the eyes of the Apollo I knew, only warmer, deeper. You'd never have known that he was a brave, adventurous, rabble-rousing god.

"Thalia, I can't imagine what you're thinking. I'm sorry I didn't express my feelings to you first, before I went to your father. I thought it was proper, and I thought, well, truth be told, I didn't think." He paused, taking my hands in his. Breathlessly he said, "While the fact is, I do think—I think of you all the time. Thalia, I've been in love with you my whole life." His deep, dark green eyes bored into mine, but I looked away. This didn't make any sense to me. We were friends, capital F.

"I—I—I," I stuttered, pulling my hands out of his and stepping back, right into a potted rhododendron. I stumbled backward, and Apollo grabbed my shoulders, pulling me upright in one powerful tug. I could feel my face turning bright red as he held on to me a moment longer than he needed to. Then he started to laugh. And I started to laugh. It wasn't really that funny, but the laughing made a lot of the tension in the air go away. And I loved to listen to Apollo laugh.

I finally caught my breath and straightened up a bit. Apollo looked at me expectantly, and I cleared my throat. "Apollo, you are my friend, my very favorite friend. I thought, well, I thought that was all. You just never let on that you felt more than friendship for me."

"Come on, Thalia. Surely you've felt it. Some part of you must have known."

"Um, no," I said. "How? Why? I mean, what makes you think you want to marry me?"

"Why," Apollo replied, shaking his head in disbelief. "You are the funniest, brightest, silliest girl I know. You are beautiful and exciting, no, thrilling, and creative. These are things that you, singularly, are to me. Not one of nine Muses, but Thalia."

Boy, he was in love. Even on my best day I'm not thrilling. Or beautiful. Cute, maybe. I looked at Apollo, really looked at him maybe for the first time ever, and realized he was the beautiful one. You've never seen lashes like his. And his skin—it was milky pure with just a splunket of rosiness at the apples of his perfectly formed cheekbones. He was perfect.

So perfect.

Too perfect.

And his lips. Come to think of it, his lips were perfect, too. I couldn't stop staring at them. But his lips weren't the point. Not at all. "A-Apollo," I stammered, trying to stay focused on why I'd come here in the first place, "I think . . . well, maybe I might . . . marry you." That was all I could get out—it was hard enough deceiving my friend. I couldn't go overboard.

"Remember that day, Thalia, the one where we hijacked Pegasus from your sister Calliope* and we took off on his back, racing through the clouds and down into Athens?" he said softly.

"How could I forget?" I said.

"It was my most favorite day ever." And as he said those seven words I thought them in my head: *It was my most favorite day ever.*

"Pegasus never saw us coming," I remembered.

"He was so stunned and didn't want to go, and then you sang to him, you sang 'Souvlaki Con Grakki' so beautifully, it was like magic, and you convinced him and that was that, and we were off. I don't have that kind of power over him. Only you."

"You teased me about it that whole day—you said that my voice cracked when I sang and that I was an evil trickster. . . ."

"Don't be foolish, Thalia. That was my way, my way of avoiding what was really on my mind. Love. Pure, incredible, soul-deep, fantastical, crazy love." He was standing closer now, his lips almost touching mine. Was he actually going to try to kiss me? I jumped back, laughing nervously.

"I like the teasing," I said, trying to gain control

---

* Calliope is my eldest, most accomplished sister.

of my spinning brain. "It's how you and I talk. I don't like this serious Apollo."

And it was true—I did like the teasing and the sarcasm. I liked it all. Apollo made me feel so good when we hung out. When we were together, I didn't feel like just one of nine Muses; I felt special and smart, and I even sometimes felt like a beautiful only child.

So what was I doing? Marrying him? Not marrying him? Lying to him! Giving myself a disease! It was too much. I felt like I was falling down some crazy spiral cloud; I felt dizzy; I felt out of control. Apollo made me feel so special and smart, and he was fun. Fun! I felt so confused. I was lying to my best friend, and for what?

Suddenly everything went black. I must've fainted because the next thing I knew I was flat on the cold, hard ground, dirty and sore. Apollo was kneeling over me, stroking my hair. "Thalia, are you okay? Thalia, Thalia!"

I looked up at those deep green eyes, eyes that looked right back at me. Eyes that were filled with worry and panic and love. I nodded to let him know I was okay and thought, I cannot do this. This couldn't be more wrong. I cannot lie to him. He's the most wonderful and beautiful person in the whole universe.

But as I lay there on the floor, my heart and head racing with confusion, Apollo continued to speak.

"Thalia, from now on you will never lift a finger

again. I will take care of you forever and ever. You can live your life as a lady, as you deserve, with no cares in the world. You will live your life like a queen."

And he went on and on with this ludicrous talk. What was making him say such things? Was he just worried about me? Did he think this drivel was what I wanted to hear? Or could this be the real Apollo? I felt truly, genuinely ill. I felt nauseous. I felt angry. He knew me better than this, didn't he? Or did he? Was his love blinding him so badly that he actually thought I wanted to live like some stuffy old queen on a hill?

Perhaps, I thought, I hit my head when I fell. This has got to be some horrible, horrendous bad dream. I shook my head hard, but Apollo was still droning on, "And you will only wear the finest lace and corsets and jewels. And you will have ladies to wait on you for everything, everything—"

"Enough!" I almost yelled. "Shush. Fine, I will marry you," I said with not so much as a smile.

TEN

It's really quite scary how you can get caught up in TV. Era, Polly, and I sat in front of it mesmerized all weekend. We watched stories about snakes in the wild, romances gone wrong, and even cooking shows. Polly liked those best. And we barely left the house. I didn't even shower. We wore our sleeping gowns all day long. It was heaven!

Still, it was nice to be back at school on Monday.

"Hey, Thalia, what are you doing tonight?" asked Claire. We had just gotten out of our last class, and the school day was officially over.

"Watching TV and eating cereal," I answered. "The usual." Isn't that sad—I'd been here only a little over a week, and already I had a "usual." Forget Polly; *I* needed a life. It didn't help that most people at school seemed to be steering clear of me, and I was sure it was thanks to the Backroom Betties.

"Wanna come with me and the boys to the Grit tonight? Pocky's gonna get up and do his one-man punk-rock-rap show. It's a riot."

"Oh, wow, I would love to, but I dunno. My sisters will probably never go for it."

"They don't have to come. Don't get me wrong, they're welcome, but you can go out without them, can't you?"

"Yeah, well, our host dad likes us to stick together. He's sort of a freak about it."

No one would understand three girls, even three exchange students, living parentally free. So, I'd learned quickly to go along with the whole exchange-host-parent thing. Even though it made me feel bad lying to Claire.

"That's cool. Well, we're going down around seven or so; it's down on Prince Street. Give me a jingle jangle if you wanna join us or just show, sweetie. We'd love to see ya. 'Specially Pocky." And then she gave me a sly smile.

"Okay," I called after her halfheartedly. "If I change my mind, I'll give you a, uh, jingle jangle."

Yikes. *Please do not let that mean Pocky has a crush on me,* I thought. Pocky is one of Claire's best friends and a funny, funny guy. *Well, looks aren't everything,* I told myself. But still.

Really, Pocky's cool. And oddly charming. He has

this awesome fuchsia Mohawk, the color of blooming bougainvillea. And a whole bunch of freckles
across his upturned nose. He's just kinda goofy and a
little clumsy and not really my type. Plus boys were
the very last thing I was interested in at the moment.

"Thalia, over here!" yelled Era. She was standing in
the middle of the quad with Polly and—and—and . . .
Tim! Hooray! I ran over.

I'd thought a lot about the Tim situation over the
weekend and had decided that my extreme faith in my
sister's taste outweighed all my misgivings about him.
He *did* have cute dimples, I told myself. And most
important, he could be our ticket to pleasing Daddy.

"Well, okay, nice talking to you, Tim. See you
tomorrow," said Polly, obviously trying to rush him
off as I arrived.

"Wait, Tim, is it? Hi, I'm Thalia."

"The alien, right?" he said, and then he laughed.

"Right, the alien, that's me," I replied, slightly
annoyed. "So, um, where do you live?"

"Thalia!" scolded Polly.

"It's a fair question," said Tim. "I live over on
Jackdaw. Between Hollings and Jennings."

"Isn't that near us? Right, isn't it, Polly?" I'd seen
those streets on our map.

Polly didn't answer me. She simply glared at me.
That piercing heart stare. Well, she could thank me
later.

"Um, would you like to walk us home? We don't live too far from you," I suggested.

Era just mouthed the word *home* over and over my way, reminding me that we couldn't exactly have people over. Besides the fact that the place was a mess (we hadn't quite mastered the whole cleaning-up-after-ourselves thing yet), it would be pretty obvious that we didn't have anyone looking after us. But Claire's parents both worked and were never around when *she* got home from school, so I thought if anyone asked, we could just say our host parents were working. Or on vacation. Or something.

"Sure, I'd be happy to," Tim replied. I wanted to go find Claire right then and there and show her—Tim wasn't a full-on poseur; he was nice. He had to be.

Polly threw me some eye daggers, and we were on our merry way.

"So, Tim, did you know that my sister Polly here has an exceptionally gorgeous voice? It's true."

"Thaliaaaaa," Polly said through gritted teeth.

"She can also play most any instrument. You play guitar, right?"

"That I do."

"Maybe you and she should collaborate, start a band, play beautiful music together."

"Oh my God, you are so dead," she whispered my way.

"It's okay, Polly. Obviously your sister is very

proud of your talents," said Tim. "I would love to hear you sing sometime. And I would love for you to hear me play. I'm rather good, if I do say so myself."

Okay, so he's a little egotistical. That never hurt anyone. Perhaps he's just confident and proud, I thought.

"I'd love to hear you sometime, Tim. I'm sure you're divine."

Polly had spoken! Thus far she had mostly just been full of trembling sighs and angry whispers. Hooray!

Maybe she needed just a bit more help. "So, Tim, Polly is also very good at writing poems. She's a master with words."

"Yes, I know, I heard her poem in class just the other day. It was quite good. Did you think mine was any good?" he asked, turning back to Polly.

"Oh yes, very good," said my sister.

"And Polly is also an incredible dancer, be it ballet, folklorico, waltzes, you name it," I added. I didn't look at her for fear of her angry stare.

"Is that so? Huh. Folklorico. What is that exactly?" he asked.

"Oh, it's nothing," Polly said all too modestly.

"It's an ancient dance—it's very intricate and graceful. She's a master," I proclaimed.

"I'm a really good dancer, too," pouted Era. I tripped her and then gave her my patented single-arched-eyebrow glare that says, "Not now." She yelped. And then pouted some more.

I fell a few steps back and yanked Era back with me so Polly and Tim could have a few moments alone and I could scold Era for not being as "thoughtful" as I was.

"What are you doing? Leave him alone—Polly likes him," I said.

"I don't want him. He's a poseur. Puh-lease. So what are you up to, anyway? You've been acting really odd around him yourself," said Era.

"He's not a poseur, and he's perfect for Polly—he likes a lot of the same things she does. She needs to find a life—you should be encouraging her."

"What, like you have been? She doesn't seem too interested in your so-called encouragement."

"Oh no? Look!" And I pointed to Polly and Tim walking a few steps in front of us, laughing and giggling and sharing an obviously rich joke.

I continued. "Polly's finding her *own* life, and I'm helping her get it, which—if I have to spell it out for you—is a selfless act." I raised my eyebrows. "So that means that we are both working on completing the tasks Daddy gave us. Have you even thought about *your* task in the past week? I'm pretty sure you've been too busy thinking about boys, as usual."

"Um, w-well . . ." Era stammered, her face softening. "I guess I kinda forgot about that," she said apologetically. "I'm going to try harder."

"I hope so." I sighed, cringing with guilt. Why had I snapped at Era like that? Sure, so she wasn't the most ambitious of us three when it came to getting home, but still.

Polly stopped. She thanked Tim for walking us home but told him we could go the rest of the way ourselves. I didn't push it. See, I know when to back off.

He thanked her for the pleasant company and kissed her hand. She turned three shades of pink.

"You know, you might enjoy coming to the Grit this evening," suggested Tim. "It's a funky little dive down on Prince. Monday's open-mike night. It's definitely a hoot. Some folks read a little poetry, sing a little. It's all very dark and hip. I think you'd really enjoy it, Polly. Plus I'll be there." And then he flashed her his pearly whites. I had to admit, they sparkled. He wasn't so incredibly clean, but his teeth sure were.

"Thanks, maybe we will see you there. Thanks again for the company," she said. Tim winked and turned on his heels. Again, not even a bye for us sisters. He was a little rude, but I'd deal.

"So, are we going?" asked Era.

"Where?" countered Polly.

"To the Grit!" said Era. "Everyone from school goes."

"Well, I guess so," said Polly, although she was

obviously more excited than she wanted to let on.

"Cool," I said. I would have to suffer the potential wrath of Pocky's crush, but it would be for a good cause—my sister's happiness. *Gosh, look at me,* I thought, perking up a little. I had become so very, very selfless in such a short amount of time. That had to count for something.

ELEVEN

We spent a lot of time primping. It was fun, too. So we didn't have handmaidens any longer—we just took turns fixing one another's hair and putting on a little makeup and helping one another pick out clothes.

We had watched a brilliant story on the TV just two days before. It talked about these models, women who get all dolled up and walk the catwalk in fabulously crazy clothes. It had inspired us that night to play with one another's hair and makeup, so now, two days later, we were all pretty good at it.

"Now, here's Polly, wearing a long plaid skirt to the floor and a man's shirt buttoned and tied, sleeves rolled. Her hair, done exclusively by Thalia, is rolled into oversized, incredibly soft curls and pulled back off her face. The shoes? Courtesy of the Greek goddess of speed, Nike.

"Enter Era, who's wearing a flirtatious little number covered in polka dots and trimmed with a sassy kick pleat. Her hair, full and natural, is filled with soft, wavy curls and falls easily down the center of her back. Her shoes are strappy and painfully pointy, and we still don't know how she walks in them.

"And then there is the vision of Thalia."

"Gosh, you're not going to let us announce you?" asked Era.

"Oh, sorry. Okay, announce me."

"And there is Thalia . . ."

"The vision of Thalia, please," I said through gritted teeth. I would have announced me better.

"And then there is the vision of Thalia. Shorter than the rest of us . . ." and then she laughed.

"C'mon, not fair, I gave you guys a great entry," I whined.

"It's not like anyone is watching," stated Era.

"Doesn't matter, c'mon."

"Okay. And there is the vision of Thalia. She is dressed in an exquisite pair of green-and-brown paisley pants that hug her petite frame effortlessly. The shirt? Why, it's an orange sweater of cashmere and something else soft and fluffy. And her shoes already look ratty and old, but she likes them; they are purple and turquoise and flat. Her hair looks divine, and why not? I did it. Pressed perfectly flat and straight in a perky bob, it is adorned with a single glittering headband."

"You look cute," said Polly.

"Thanks, I think."

"So let's go, let's go, let's go, let's go!" said Era.

We were off on our first real night out in Georgia. And we were going to ride in one of those racy chariots.

Honk, honk!

"That's Claire—come on!"

I grabbed a small stack of the money under the sink, and we all made a run for the door.

"Hop in," said Claire. Pocky and Hammerhead were already filling up the backseat. I ran around to the front and got in next to Claire. Polly followed and sat next to me, and Era carefully climbed in next to Hammerhead. With a slam of the door, we were off.

"So, like, the big guy eased up on you all, huh?" asked Claire.

Before I had time to answer for us, Era said, "Oh, Zeus would want us here."

"Zeus?"

"Um, Jesús. He's, uh, Spanish," I covered.

"You should let me meet him. Daddies love me," boasted Pocky.

"Um, yeah, maybe sometime. He changed his mind and thought we should get out more," I explained.

"So, Thalia, you will never be able to get rid of me now. I know where you live," said Pocky quietly.

I smiled and laughed nervously.

"He's just messing with you, Thalia, don't take him seriously. I know you dig that poseur dude, and that's cool, you know—I thought about it and . . ."

"Ix-nay on the oseur-pay."

"Oh, you got that pig-Latin thing down, girl," said Claire.

"What's she talking about, Thalia—do you like someone?" asked Polly.

"*No!*" I yelped.

"Whoa, it better be me, sweetheart—please let it be me," Pocky said again.

"*No!*" I yelled.

Claire went on. "I just want you to know that as your friend, I thought I had to warn you, but—"

"*No!*" I screamed.

Just then Hammerhead started to hum this awful tune, louder and louder. Everyone stopped focusing on me to focus on him.

"Dude, stop!" yelled Pocky.

"Thanks, Hammer," I said, very, very quietly.

"No prob, Thalia," countered Hammerhead even more softly. Hammerhead didn't ever say that much, but he always seemed to know what was going on.

A little more bickering back and forth and we were at the Grit.

The room was totally dark with these red lanterns glowing in every corner. It wasn't exactly clean. But it did have this deep, I'm-on-an-adventure sorta smell that I liked.

"Hey, Thalia." A gal from my algebra class waved. I waved back and smiled. Another girl, this one from my phys-ed class, waved and said, "Yo." All in all, I saw, like, seven people from my classes, most of whom said hello. Two girls, who I recognized from the group of Backroom Betty groupies, just laughed. But I didn't care. I felt cool. I felt happening. I felt with it.

"Hey, beautiful, come watch me perform." I felt dorky. It was Pocky, breathing down my neck.

I latched on to Era and Polly. Polly's eyes were darting everywhere through the darkness, looking for Tim. We three sat down, Claire followed, and Pocky took the stage. It was just him and this guy named Guy up there. Guy had a ratty old guitar that plugged in. Pocky just held this small black object in his hand that made his voice sound extra loud.

"Hey, that thing's pretty cool," I said to Claire, pointing to the object. "What is it?"

"You mean the microphone? The mike?" she asked, laughing.

"Um, yeah. I was just wondering what kind of . . . mike . . . it was." Claire gave me a weird look and just shrugged.

"I wrote this song for the most beautiful girl at school," Pocky boomed over the mike, directing his gaze at me. "The one and only Thalia Moose."

Everyone looked at me. I gasped. Era kicked me, and Polly just chuckled.

Pocky wailed:

> "She's the vision of a goddess
> Out of Greek mythology,
> I want to hold her in my arms,
> I want to practice biology. . . ."

I stiffened. Was this his way of telling me he knew who I was? What I was? Before I had a chance to say anything to my sisters, Guy started strumming the guitar frantically. Pocky screamed over the noise, "Thalia! Thalia! Thalia!" for probably three minutes, and then the song was over.

Claire tried to comfort me. "Don't be too alarmed, Thalia. Whenever a new girl comes to town, he sings the same song for them, only he repeats their name instead of yours. Pocky is his own little welcome committee."

"Okay, great. Right."

And then out of nowhere appeared Polly's prince. Well, it was Tim. He took a seat next to her and flashed us all his extremely white teeth. In this light they pretty much glowed. "Thalia, it seems you have an admirer." And then he paused for dramatic effect. "As does your sister." And then he turned toward Polly and fluttered his eyelashes. It was a bit much, but whatever. All that mattered was that Polly got her guy. And it certainly looked like she was getting him. They started whispering things into each other's ears. And I tried to feel happy for them.

"I get to do one mo', right?"

It was Pocky talking in this weird accent, asking no one in particular.

No one in particular answered him, so he started. "One and a two and a . . ." Guy started strumming slowly, and this time Pocky sang instead of shouting, "More than a woman, more than a woman to me . . . More than a woman, more than a woman to me."

And then he rapped:

> "She's a fine little lady,
> Makes me feel a little shady,
> She's so cute and squeaky,
> And I'm just a little freaky.
> Let me take you for sukiyaki,
> Then you'll want a little Pocky,
> She's the one they call Thalia,
> And she's surely gonna wow ya."

And then he started singing that more-than-a-woman thing again.

"Now, this one, this one is all you and totally new," said Claire.

"Great."

"I think it's kinda sweet, Thalia. That was one fine rap," offered up Tim.

"Yep, nobody's every rhymed *Thalia* with *wow ya* before," I said.

"Exactly," Tim said absently, and then he went back to cooing in my sister's ear.

Pocky made his way over to the table. "What'd you think, Thalia?"

"I'm immensely flattered, Pocky, really, very flattered."

"And . . ."

"And you were really good. Really, very good."

"And . . ."

"And, um, Guy was good, too."

"And . . ."

"Oh, give her a break, Pocky!" said Claire.

"And . . . you want me now, don't you?" he continued.

"Um, no, but I'm immensely flattered. Really very good, Guy, too."

"That's cool." And he flopped down next to me at the table. Pocky is a man who rolls with the punches.

It was going to be a few minutes before another performer took the stage, so Polly and Era hit the bathrooms. I stayed at the table, drinking my Coke (which was sweet and syrupy and delicious, by the way) and making small talk with Pocky and Claire. After a few moments of listening to us speak passionately on the topic of fried potatoes with cheese, which I had, amazingly, learned to cook the night before, Tim excused himself and said he, too, had to go to the bathroom. Claire started pointing out all the boys she thought were cute, most of whom were not from our school.

The conversation turned to tastes in boys. When Claire asked me what I liked in a guy, I just couldn't shake this visual of Apollo's sly little sideways grin. I must've gotten lost in it because the next thing I knew, Claire was summoning me back to earth.

"What was that little brain freeze about?" she asked.

"Nothing, really. A boy back home. Old home. Old boy. Never mind. Really. That guy in back of us, Claire, he looks like your type, no?"

And Claire was off again, talking about this boy and that. After several minutes neither my sisters nor Tim had returned to the table. Then Claire said, "Oh, look, it's Teri, one of your favorite girls." I followed Claire's gaze. Yep, there was the head Backroom Betty. And she was talking to Tim.

Frozen, I watched as the two of them whispered and giggled and Tim leaned in, close, closer, closest, until I could feel my blood rising to the surface of my skin. Tim jerked a finger toward the girls' bathroom, and they both laughed. That was it. I had to say something, anything. I had to find out what they were talking about because it looked like it had to do with Polly. I got up and walked in their direction, weaving through the crowd.

Claire called after me, "Thalia, what are you doing?" but I didn't listen.

I crossed the club, but by the time I reached Tim, Teri was gone. I looked around, but I couldn't figure out where she'd disappeared to.

"Who were you just talking to?" I asked accusingly.

"Excuse me?" he asked back.

"Who were you just talking to?"

"You mean Teri? A friend. Why? What's the problem?" And then he smiled his slickest of smiles.

"You should pick better ones."

"Excuse me?" Tim said, still grinning. I started to tell him how cruel the Backroom Betties had been to me and my sisters and how evil they were. But he acted like he couldn't hear me over the din of the club.

Just then my sisters emerged from the bathroom, and Tim slid his arm around Polly's waist. I felt like heaving. He'd looked awfully cozy with Teri just moments before. And now he was sidling up to my sister.

"Let's sit down, Polly. I want to hear more about your music," he said.

Okay, so maybe Tim had just been *talking* to that girl. But I couldn't shake the feeling that something was not right. Still, I had to face it—I had little experience in the relationship arena. My only knowledge, real knowledge, of boys was of Apollo. And he would never, not then and I'm sure not now, flirt with other girls when I wasn't looking. I was his best friend and the center of his attentions. Apollo always put me first, even when I didn't want to be. He teased me, for sure, but he always looked out for me.

Tim better be worth all this headache, I thought. *He better be truly interested in my sister.* He just had to be.

Maybe it was just a mistake. Being friends with Teri, that is—maybe Tim just didn't know how mean she really was. I mean, anyone can make a mistake, right? Even Apollo, the perfect Apollo, made a *huge* one, with all that talk about treating me like a queen. That still doesn't make him a bad person.

But, of course, I wasn't quite so understanding in his case. . . .

TWELVE

"Corsets! Corsets? Can you believe he actually said, 'You will wear corsets'? What the heck has come over him? I wouldn't wear a corset if someone paid me all the gold gumdrops and purple dandelions in the world. Doesn't he know how utterly uncomfortable those things are?" Era and Polly and I were, once again, in the Beautorium. I'd just finished telling them about my conversation with Apollo in the garden.

I didn't tell them how I had almost, almost called off our plan. I didn't tell them that for a brief moment, I'd thought of nothing else but Apollo's perfect rosy pout.

"Calm down. You're not actually going to marry him," Polly reminded me. "You don't have to face a future in corsets just yet."

"Shhh, here come our ladies. They don't need to know of our plans," said Era.

Polly, Era, and I had gathered in the West Wing of the Beautorium, the room specially reserved for gown fittings. In a few days, I thought, everyone would know of our deceit. The thought did make me feel slightly fearful and worried on account of Apollo's feelings. And there was sure to be an aftermath of some kind. But I'd dealt with my father's anger before. I'd been punished for tying Hermes's golden shoelaces together. (I was nine, he took a tiny spill, and I had to wear donkey ears for three weeks.) I'd been reprimanded for conspiring with my cousin Dionysus* to make Hera think she was losing her mind. Now, that was worth it. Daddy spared me that time, and Dion, well, Hera made him go mad for real. All I had to do was scrub walls for three days and three nights in Poseidon's castle, deep under the sea. It was kinda cool, actually. The freaky sea fishes, not the nasty barnacle busting.

Then there was the time Apollo and I took Pegasus to earth. All the punishment in the world would have been worth that day. We stayed out all night, too. Whoa, was Daddy mad. Hera, I think, was secretly thrilled. Daddy said I couldn't see Apollo for five whole months. I was devastated. But then time flew by. Literally, time flew on by my window and the five months were over, just like that! Apollo is a very powerful god. He tossed a

---

* Dion just wandered the world, screaming and yelling at anyone who listened. He sort of became a drunk after that.

spell on Father Time to fly 379 times faster than he usually does. My dad missed the whole thing because he and
Hera were off vacationing in Troy.

Those were the days. When Apollo and I were
happy and normal and he showed me he cared by teasing me and taking me on adventures. And maybe as
we got older, we flirted. A little. But it was a harmless
flirtation, not an overly dramatic romance.

All my thoughts of Apollo were interrupted by our
ladies-in-waiting, who were carrying in these huge poofy
dresses. And to think these things were just for the
engagement party. Polly must have sensed my fear, for
she whispered in my ear, "Just this once, for the party."

Era was actually looking enviously at the enormous
ball of foof that I was currently attempting to fit into.
"It's so lovely. This is the very best part of weddings,
don't you think?" she gushed. Polly shot Era a look
that all but said, "Can it!"

"Well, I think you'll be needing a corset, Miss
Thalia; this dress is just a wee bit tight," said Lenora,
my personal lady-in-waiting. Oh, wasn't that rich! Not
even married yet, and Apollo had gotten me in corsets
just like he wanted.

I wanted to whine, to scream, to wail, "Noooooooo!"
But Polly gave me that look, the one she had flashed Era
moments ago, the one that said, "Can it!" Only when she
glanced my way, her face was far softer and deeply more
understanding.

It didn't matter, anyway; I couldn't say no to Lenora. She had known me since I was born. Lenora had dressed my mother before me. Sure, she never smiled, and her skin was brittle and cracked, and she wasn't too huggable, but she loved me.

By this time Lenora had me stitched and sewn up so tight, I could barely breathe. Or talk.

"Pol, wat-er, pwease."

"Lenora, can you ease up a bit? She can't even speak right," said Polly.

"Right, milady." But she really didn't loosen those strings all that much. I still could feel my morning brekkie of ambrosia creeping up my throat.

"Well, I think you look divine," gushed Era.

"And so do we," said three familiar voices behind me. I couldn't turn myself, so Lenora spun me around on the giant lazy Susan I was standing on, revealing my three least-favorite girls in all of the universe: Tizzie, Alek, and Meg, aka the Furies.

"What do you three want?" asked my sister, her voice dripping with dislike.

"We came to call a truce on the eve of your wedding, Thalia," said Alek, the one I think I hated the most. She had tortured me when we were children, called me names that were inconceivable, embarrassed me in front of all the heavens—she had even made me eat dirt once. Even when it's fancied up with marshmallows, dirt doesn't taste good, in case you were wondering.

"Please accept our apologies for all that kid stuff. We're adults now; we should act as such," said Tizzie, her hair a brilliant shade of orange.

Thing was, I wasn't an adult. This marriage stuff didn't change that. And these girls, these girls were definitely not adults. Why, just last week my sister Clio was outside with her beau and she thought she spotted Meg behind a tree. She went and looked behind the tree, but there was no Meg. Only a giant vat of fish heads, which promptly fell on her head. It was a pointless, silly, and mean little trick, the kind only a child plays.

Adult shmadult.

"Pretty scarf," said Era to Alek. Era takes people at their word. So if Alek said she came in peace, Era believed it. She obviously thought she would make nice with a compliment. Me, I'm not convinced so easily.

"Thank you," said Alek. "It was a gift from Jason."*

I told you they were up to no good. The Furies knew darn well that Jason was Era's crush of the month. That was a little jab thrown directly at my sister's heart. They couldn't even control themselves for five minutes.

"Oh, well, it's beautiful," said Era, her lip a-quivering.

"We come with a prewedding gift for you, Thalia," said Tizzie.

---

* A serious babe and heir to the throne of Greece. He's sort of the Prince William of ancient times.

"Would it be a tiara of poisonous snakes or maybe a bracelet made of sharp shards of glass?" I asked.

"Thalia!" scolded Lenora. "You apologize at once. They come in peace."

Oh, great, they've got Lenora hoodwinked.

"Yes, ma'am. I'm oh, so terribly, ridiculously, apologetically, resolutely sorry, girls," I said.

"Enough," said Lenora through gritted teeth.

"Look, we come bearing gifts," said Meg. "An ancient perfume oil from the nether reaches of the deep blue sea. It smells of purple and yellow sea lilies."

The perfume she held out to me was in this gorgeous bottle all adorned in glitter and gold. That was one of the cruddiest things about the Furies—they always had the best stuff.

"Take the gift, Thalia, and thank your visitors," said Lenora.

"Yes, ma'am. Thank you, thank you so very much. I will treasure this gift always. . . ."

The Furies, in unison, said, "You are most welcome," and then turned on their heels and left.

"Don't touch it!" said Polly as soon as they were gone. "It's got to be a trick."

"Oh, you girls are far too suspicious," said Lenora. "Those young girls are harmless. They came in peace. Let's have a whiff of that old stuff."

"I'm dying to smell it!" said Era, her eyes as wide as they could be.

"I don't know. I don't trust them. Not one bit. Still, that bottle is exquisite looking," said Polly.

"I just want to smell it," said Era. "I'm sure it's harmless."

"No!" screamed Polly and I in unison.

But Era opened the bottle and nothing came out. No demons, no snakes, no spiders.

I put my nose to the bottle and took a sniff. Oh. I was taken aback—this was truly the most gorgeous smell I had ever smelled, a smell so fabulously smelly, all I could do was yell at Polly, "Smell!" and with that, I thrust the bottle out to her.

Polly smelled, and nothing bad happened to her, either. We swooned at the ripeness and plumpness of the perfume. It was, without a doubt, heavenly.

"Okay, maybe they weren't up to anything," said Polly, still smiling from the sweet intensity of the perfume.

"See," said Lenora.

I dabbed a touch on my wrist and another drop or two behind my ears.

I actually felt a little bad about taking a wedding gift knowing full well I didn't intend on getting married at all. Then I got another whiff of the ancient sea lilies, and I didn't feel that bad at all. Not at all.

I should have listened to the little voice inside me that told me nothing involving the Furies could *possibly come to good. But I ignored that voice. I ignored a lot of things I should have paid more attention to. . . .*

✻ ✻ ✻

Oh, Thalia, you make this much too easy for us,
To fool you and your sisters wasn't much fuss.
We put a minor spell on old Lenora, you see,
Then she backed us up like a faithful chimpanzee.
That perfume you think smells so divine
Is filled with a mutant form of ol' strychnine.
Like we said before, Scyllia will befall
the first person Thalia touches at her very fine ball.
All thanks to the ancient sea lily perfume,
Tomorrow she'll have a forever green groom!
One that slobbers and oozes and drips, don't you know,
With an ugly third eye where there should be a nose!
And who will the finger of blame be pointed at?
Our own little Thalia—a tit for a tat!

✻ ✻ ✻

THIRTEEN

Back in our little house in Georgia, Polly tiptoed into my room. All quiet, like a castle mouse hiding from a guard. But I wasn't sleeping. I was wondering if Tim really liked that evil Backroom Betty and how life on earth wasn't all adventure and escapades; it was a whole lotta headache.

"I'm awake," I said in a whisper.

"Oh, good. I wanted to talk. Can I get in bed with you?"

"Well, it's not that I don't want you to, but have you noticed where I sleep, Polly? This tub isn't exactly big enough for the both of us."

"But I need some sisterly bonding," she said in her sweetest, most sugary voice.

"Okay, okay, get in."

She climbed into my tub, her feet to my head and my head to her feet, and got under the comforter I had stolen from Era's bed. My little sister is hot-blooded; she didn't really need much in the way of blankets, anyway.

"I just wanted to thank you for your support with this whole Tim thing. I know I pooh-poohed you at first and told you not to bother, but . . ."

"You did more than tell me not to bother—you threatened me. But that's cool."

"Yeah, that; I'm sorry. I really, truly appreciate what you've done, helping out. I really think I, well, perhaps I do like him. Can you believe it? He asked me to write this song with him. I've put a lot of time into it, and I think it's going to be really quite good. We're going to perform it at open-mike night at the Grit. Isn't that wonderful?"

"Yeah, Polly, that's great."

But I wasn't so sure. I couldn't shake the sinking feeling that Tim was gonna turn out to be a low-down, dirty perpetrator in need of a swift kick in the . . . Whoa. I was getting carried away. Polly really liked him, and they were spending some quality time together. She knew him better than I. Yes, I thought, she did know him better, and there was easily, surely, positively a reasonable explanation for what I had seen the other night. Flirting shmirting—Tim was probably just a seriously social guy. The kind of person who gets along with anyone and everyone. He was just being friendly.

"So, last night, late, I wrote a poem. A sort of,

well, maybe like a love poem."

I didn't say anything. The word *speechless* came to mind.

"Thalia, what is it? Do you think I'm insane? I don't know, he tells me all sorts of things, like how beautiful he thinks my voice is and how smart I am, and, well, I just love the way I feel when I am with him—it's wildly new and . . ."

"You are all those things and more, and you don't need to hear them from other people to feel good about yourself, Polly."

"It's not that," she said. "I just, well, I like to hear them from him."

"That's great—no, that's really good. It's a great feeling, right? You feel good, no?"

"I feel great. I can't believe I am going to say this out loud, but this was the best punishment in the whole wide universe. I love earth, and I'm so glad we're here, together."

"Yeah, me too."

I thought of my greater need for selflessness and I thought of Daddy telling me I needed to shape up and I thought of Apollo's sad eyes and I thought of Polly's radiant smile and even though I thought of Tim's flirtatiousness with that horrible girl from science, I said, "So why don't you give him the love poem?"

"Oh no! I wrote it for me, not him, not really. I mean, I have these feelings, I mean, I get all tingly and I would love to share that with him, these new feelings and thoughts and, well, no, I couldn't."

"Why not? He obviously adores you. And why shouldn't he? You're truly the most stunning and fascinating girl at school. A veritable goddess!" I said, and I meant it. Well, I meant the part about her being stunning and fascinating and a real-life goddess.

"Nooo," she said slyly, coyly, quietly. But I could see her mind was at work. I couldn't help but egg her on. She giggled those rippling little happy giggles that come uncontrollably from the throat and then leaned over and gave me the tightest hug. She was so happy.

"You have to give it to him. How can you hide your feelings? How can you play such high school games? Just trust in your judgment. I do," I said.

"Maybe, yes, maybe," she said with the sweetest smile yet.

Then she lay back and closed her eyes.

She was going to sleep in my tub?!

This setup was fine for sister bonding, but c'mon, it was hard, cold, and not all that big.

"Yo, Pol, you really going to sleep in here?"

"I was thinking about it. Yeah," she said, her eyes still closed, her mouth still frozen in midsmile.

"Um, okay. Good night," I replied sullenly.

I must be more selfless, I must be more selfless, I must be more selfless, I chanted mentally till the ache in my back faded away into deep and restful slumber.

FOURTEEN

"You know, Pocky really is harmless," Claire said as she sat down next to me on the damp grass in the middle of the quad. It was lunchtime.

"I know, don't even worry about it," I said. "That stuff, those songs, they were pretty funny. I got a kick out of it."

"Yeah, that Pocky, he's a hoot."

Eating with Claire was the best. She never brought the same thing twice. And she always had a blanket to set her food out on and real shiny silverware. She, too, made her own lunches, but while I stuck to basics like cheese and bread, Claire fashioned these marvels out of food. Last week she had made a peanut butter and jelly sandwich, but with cake for the bread. It was the size of a large dictionary. Today's meal consisted of a sprinkle sandwich and pink popcorn. And of course the best part was, she always shared.

"So what did you get on Mr. Zeitland's paper?" asked Claire.

"An A. It was pretty cool."

"You, Thalia, are exceptionally talented in the world of science. Why is that?"

"What do you mean?"

"You're good at it. You're good at school. Is this school just so much easier than your old school or what?"

"Um, it's just real different?" I said.

"Different how?"

"Well, for one thing, I never had to deal with the whole note-passing issue before I came to Georgia. Not to say we didn't have our share of witchy girls or dopey boys, but, I dunno, I didn't have to see them, like, every day."

"Yeah, well, the witch quotient went up here exponentially when the Backroom Betties came along a couple of weeks ago."

Something about what Claire had just said made my blood run cold. "What do you mean? They haven't been here for, like, aeons? When did they come to this school?" I asked.

"Just like a week before you three got here. They fit in alongside the jocks and the cheerleaders right quick. It's funny that Teri was just hanging all over Tim at the Grit last night. When she first got here, he made a beeline straight for her, and she wouldn't give him the time of day. Now look at her. Batting those big blue eyes." Claire nodded to a spot across the quad.

And it was true, there was Teri cooing at none other than Tim Rhys himself as he serenaded her on his guitar. And *he* was definitely serenading her, that—that—that witch and that poseur-playing snitch!

"Your sister is just so much way cooler than that chick." Apparently she'd figured out that it wasn't me who had the crush on Tim. "Well, I warned you, he's a poseur." But I hardly heard her.

"Argh!"

I watched in horror as Teri leaned over and kissed Tim on the cheek. I couldn't take it. I got up and marched directly over to the two of them and asked him squarely to his face, "What the heck is your problem?"

"What the heck? What the heck? Are you nine? Jeez, Thalia, chill."

"Um, chill? Chill? What on earth does that mean? What about my sister?"

He just laughed, laughed at me, and shrugged.

"Thalia?" Teri said in a smooth voice that made me want to explode. "It's very sweet that you're worried about your sister. But can't you see that Tim and I are busy?"

I was speechless. Or virtually. "Ah, wha, pla," was all I said. It was all I could do not to turn them both into slugs right then and there in the middle of the school quad.

"Look, Thalia, your sister's all right, but honestly, dude, she ain't pulling her weight on this project we got going on. I mean, I'm an artist, and I need to work constantly on my art, and Teri here is giving me feedback on my tune, which really is more than I can say for your sister."

"You are a goat-faced little liar," I yelled.

But they both just laughed. An infuriating, self-satisfied grin never left Teri's face.

"Look, I got to be done with this by tomorrow, so can you leave me alone so I can finish my song?" said Tim.

His song? His song! Tim was quite possibly the biggest jerk I had ever encountered, and that's saying a lot since I have known many, many jerks.*

I walked away, feeling helpless and powerless. What was I going to do?

More important, what was I going to say to Polly?

---

* Olympus is filled with them, each one more horrible than the next, killing their mothers and sacrificing their daughters. The heavens are rough.

FIFTEEN

Both Era and Polly were waiting for me at our spot after school.

"Why are you here, Polly? I thought you had practice with Tim," I said. I'd really been hoping that I wouldn't even have a chance to talk to her till tomorrow. I needed time to formulate my plan. But then I noticed that Polly didn't look so hot.

"I gave him my poem at the beginning of class, and he just took it from me and sort of grunted," Polly said in a shaky half whisper. "It was so odd. And then after class he just left. He started to walk down the hall with that horrible girl Teri, and he just left me standing there. I called to him, but nothing, he didn't even turn around. I don't understand. I thought he liked me. I should have never given him that poem, *never*!"

And then my beautiful, strong, oft-silent sister burst out into a chorus of off-key tears.

We walked, and she sobbed alongside us. I wondered what boy in his right mind would reject my sister's love.

"Look, I don't know what is up, but there has to be a reasonable explanation for this," I said, rather reasonably, I might add. "What that is, right now, just remains to be seen."

"I can tell you what it is," said Polly between gasps of air. "He doesn't like me. He got to know me and found out I am not worthyyyyy." And with that she let out a long and painful wail.

"That's just downright silly," said Era.

"Era's right," I concurred. "That's more than silly. That's hilariously wrong. And on so many levels."

"Well, then, explain it to me. Someone? It's so obvious, and the only reason you two don't see it is because you are my sisters. But face it, I have been completely unsuccessful at this whole earth-in-the-future school thing. I can't even get one earth boy to like me. I'm a big, fat failure, and now what, now what?" And she sobbed some more.

"Well, if it makes you feel any better, so am I," said Era.

I tried to get her to stop. "I don't think that will make anyone feel better, Era," I said through gritted teeth.

"Oh, and how are you a failure, Era, too many boys looking your way as you cruise down the halls?" Polly said, her face turning a pale shade of jealous green.

"See, I told you it wouldn't make anyone feel any better, Era!"

"No, I'm serious. I'm a complete and total failure," Era went on. "I haven't done one thing on my own yet. I've just been thinking about boys and talking to boys and talking about boys, and not that that's not fun and all, but I really kind of want to go home, and I just have no willpower whatsoever. And it doesn't help to have everyone thinking that I'm the circus-freak alien clown's sister. In fact, I think, no, I know, that not nearly as many boys have been checking me out as there were last week." Era's eyes started to well up with tears.

I scowled at her, but Polly, my ever caring sister, was so moved by our sister's tears that she instantly became distracted by Era's problems. Which helped her quickly to forget her own.

She comforted Era, who was now sniffling along at a snail's pace. "Hmmm, I wonder if it *is* because of Thalia," said Polly.

"Hello, I'm here, please don't talk about me like I'm not. I didn't do anything that would make people dislike me or call me a freak or an alien. I didn't!" I whined.

At that point I thought I might as well throw all my sorrows into the pot and *really* distract the group. "Well, at least you don't have a Mohawked, plaid-wearing, five-foot-tall boy following you around, serenading you with off-key tunes wherein he rhymes *Thalia* with *Taco Bell Value*."

That got a smile out of them.

"I mean, what if you two had someone trailing your every move," I said, and then I affected Pocky's faux gangsta accent. "'No one is as spicy as the hottest sister Era—next to her, chilis are weak, even the fiery habanera!'"

That got a few giggles out of them. I had to please my audience. I continued, "With her hair golden soft and her drawl so sugary sweet, her singing voice will make lorikeets go into superheat."

More smiles, more laughter.

"Do Polly, do Polly," cried Era, wiping at her nose with her sleeve.

"Okay." I thought for a moment. "But no one is as enchanting as the fair sister Polly—she is as pretty as the rare tigers of Bengali."

Now they were really hysterical. They were still clinging to each other, in that clutched pose two sisters walk in when they comfort each other, but now they were rife with the giggles.

"For the sister who is smartest and cleverest of the

pack—she deserves a ride home on a Rhodesian Ridgeback!" My sisters laughed and laughed.

And then for my big finale, I took the stance of Pocky, my back arched forward, my hands moving quickly around me with no apparent purpose. "Boys are often clueless, boys are often lame—they can't recognize a bad apple from a classy dame, but the worst one among them is the brownnoser, who goes by the name of hairy Tim the poseur."

My sister's face just went white. And then the flood of tears. I had gone too far.

"I'm sorry, I didn't mean to make you upset—I was being funny. Ha, ha? Oh, Polly, I am so sorry."

"Waaahhhhhhhhh," cried Polly.

And with that, my short-lived career as an international rap star was over before it had begun.

SIXTEEN

Well, the one thing I could say for the next day was that it was Friday. Which meant that we'd soon have two whole days off before we had to be back in this little slice of Hades we were stuck in.

Was I bitter this morning? You betcha, by golly.

I really didn't feel like being here today. A few people said hi to me, but it was beginning to dawn on me that the people at my new school, though they were mostly pretty nice, were still strangers. And some of them, the group of kids that always hung out with the Backroom Betties, were just downright rude. Claire was out—she and her mom had gone to visit her grandma for the weekend a day early. Pocky wasn't anywhere to be found. I felt very alone.

That was until lunch, where, since it was Friday (hallelujah), I got to see my sisters.

We found a small, quiet corner of the quad and sat down. Polly hardly ate at all; she just stared at her plate. And I nibbled on my bologna sandwich half-heartedly. Earth food was really starting to bore me. In fact, earth was starting to bore me, period.

Well, maybe that wasn't quite right. It wasn't boredom that had me so down this morning. It was frustration. Sometime between Tuesday and today, Polly had closed herself up like a giant clam. She now looked even more miserable than when we got here. And Era, well, Era was depressed because of Polly. And me? I was completely confused. How could Tim have turned out to be such a jerk? It was so unfair.

I looked at my two sisters and felt that old guilt creep back up on me, the guilt for getting them into this mess. I had to get us out of it. I just *had* to.

I pasted a huge, what I hoped was a genuine, smile on my face. "Okay, look, so Tim isn't such a great guy. Right? Right. Well, who knew? Anyway, who cares? I mean, after all, boys aren't important, anyway, right?" Polly and Era looked at me dubiously, and Polly bit from her sandwich as if it were sandpaper. "I mean, other than Tim, things are pretty good. It could be worse, right? We just need to refocus our efforts, and we'll be back home in Olympus before you can say—"

The sound of the PA system cut me off. It rang with this awful feedback noise, something akin to Guy's guitar last Monday at the Grit. Then a familiar voice came on the loudspeaker. "Attention, attention, everyone. I just wanted to read to you a masterful piece of art written by one of our very own Nova High students. . . ." It was Tim, his voice dripping with sarcasm.

"It begins, 'Dearest Tim.'"

My heart sank down into my gut of bologna.

"'To this world I came a little gun shy,
Your voice, your song, are my life's lullaby.
You became the familiar in a sea of unknown,
My heart quivers with ache deep
in my breastbone . . .'"

Era was wincing. Polly's eyes welled up with tears. She just sat there, frozen in midbite.

"'. . . for it is you, Tim, who makes me feel at ease,
And for you it is true, I wish to please,
Because I am Polly, I can be your sweet muse
your dancer, your scribe, your sweetest chanteuse. . . .'"

The quad echoed with intense cheers and loud guffaws.

That's when Polly got up and ran. Ran so fast, the heel on her shoe broke off and she went up in the air. Half-chewed bologna came flying out of her mouth, and she landed with a crunching thud right on the concrete in front of the Backroom Bettys' own little bench, which was, luckily (or so I thought at the time), empty. The laughter was deafening. The whole school roared with a huge hurrah.

Polly's face was flushed beyond any recognition; her knees were both bloody with scrapes and filthy with ground-in dirt. I'd never seen any one of my sisters bleed before. It was horrifying. Era and I both jumped up simultaneously and dashed toward her, but before we even got close, she was up and running again. This time she was successful in getting out of the quad, out of the school, out of Dodge.

Era and I rushed back to our bench and collected our things as well as Polly's books and bag. We could feel everyone's eyes on us as they whispered and giggled. The whole school just buzzed, drowning out the last few lines of Polly's poem, which was booming over the loudspeaker. And then the poem ended, and we heard Tim's laugh, his unmistakable skanky, smarmy laugh echoing against the walls, louder than anything else.

As Era and I rushed through the halls, I was already planning what I was going to do to Tim when I next saw him. But then I heard another laugh ring out over the PA, and my heart just froze. And suddenly I knew why the Backroom Betties hadn't been sitting in their usual spot at lunch. The laugh was made up of three voices, in fact. Three fiercely familiar female chuckles. Three fiercely familiar *evil* female chuckles.

SEVENTEEN

Late that night Polly was still crying. She had come home, taken off her broken shoes, and climbed up the old oak tree that lived behind our house. There she sat, sobbing.

I climbed up first. Then Era. We sat up there, cradled by the branches, staring up into the black sky that was completely lit up with brilliant teeny-tiny intense stars. The craggy branch I was perched on was, in fact, as comfortable as my bed, the bathtub.

"This reminds me of home," said Polly, speaking of the tree and the stars and the evening's fragrant breezes.

"Me too," said Era, herself looking mildly depressed.

"So let's go over this again, one more time, okay?" I said. I got nods, as much an approval to continue as either of them had in them.

"Tim is a self-important, deceitful little boy with a

bad haircut. Polly, on the other hand, is an insanely bright, astonishingly talented, and all-around gorgeous *goddess*. Do you read me?"

"Yes, Thalia," Polly said with little enthusiasm. I wanted enthusiasm.

"Look, the fact is, we're all three incredibly smart girls. We've got years and years, decades, heck, millenniums ahead of us to live. Does living life really need to include pining over foolish boys who don't understand our ways? Do we care what people think of us, really, in the big picture? Forget about high school and boys—we don't need 'em; we can be what we want to be. We can go where we want to go. . . ."

"I want to go back home and I can't. Explain that one," said Era.

"But we're still young—that's my point! So we're stuck here for now, but it is the future that we can aspire to. Next week, next month, this won't mean anything. What matters is that we have our friends and each other and our future, our potential."

But my incredibly inspirational speech wasn't having much of an effect on anyone, myself included. I hated the idea that people were laughing and whispering about us, and I, too, wanted to go home.

"It's not just Tim, Thalia," Polly whispered. "It's just that I've been thinking a great deal about what Daddy said. About my need to live my own life. Not by finding it in books or through fixing the lives of others, but by finding it in myself. And I guess I thought that being in love would make that happen somehow. But now I wonder if that's not true. Maybe I can't change who I am. Maybe none of us can. Maybe you can never be selfless and Era can never stop being so easily swayed. Maybe we'll never get to go home." Polly paused to swipe at a stray tear, which was dribbling down her nose. "And for a while, I was even thinking that maybe that wouldn't be so bad. But now all I want is to get out of this place. And I am surely, certainly never going back to school ever again."

Polly was right. I'd thought earth would be different somehow. I'd thought we could really change. But maybe we couldn't. And I surely didn't want to be here anymore. Not after today, not after seeing all of those people laugh at my sister. I missed home.

And I missed Apollo. The way he would fight with me about such things as music or sports. The way he talked with me. No one here really talked *with* me, besides my sisters. My only friend here was Claire, and while she was outrageously cool, she didn't truly know me or know who I was, and I certainly couldn't tell her anything. Even if I could have, no one could take the place of Apollo.

Life on earth kind of sucked.

Polly's tears eventually stopped, but we stayed in the tree, just talking about home. Era talked about running around the garden mazes barefoot with every teenage midlevel god chasing behind her. Polly spoke of her favorite spot, behind the Beautorium, where the cashmere rabbits would cool themselves in the shade of the wisteria tree. And me, all I could think about was how I had, yet again, put myself and my own concerns and my own agenda ahead of everyone else's. Yes, I had wanted to make Polly happy, but not just for her own sake. No, I'd thought that if I proved I could help, I, Thalia, one of the nine Muses of Helicon, could prove I was selfless. And in trying to do so, I had proved exactly the darn opposite.

Hey, isn't recognizing your faults half the battle?

I lay back, closed my eyes, and chanted silently to myself, *I must be more selfless, I must be more selfless, I must be more selfless.* But my mind did not go blank with fabulous selfless thoughts. It went straight back to Apollo and his sweet, sexy smile. And that night. The night I ruined everything . . .

EIGHTEEN

"I can't believe I'm going to do this," I said through tightly clenched teeth as my eight sisters and I waited for our introduction.

"You have no other choice, do you?" said, or sort of asked, Polly.

When we heard Daddy announce us, we stepped out from behind the curtain and onto the stage. I looked around and saw that everyone was there. My sister Clio had thrown a truly wonderful party. If only it was celebrating a happy occasion. I put my best face on as I moved forward.

The nine of us took nine steps more. And then my father held out his hand, which signaled for me to leave the lineup and come to the edge of the stage.

I didn't see Apollo at first. My eyes darted

everywhere, looking for him. I quickly became more anxious; my palms started to sweat.

Then I saw him.

His smile was soft; his eyes were focused and bright. When my father nodded, Apollo walked up the stairs and took my fingers in his trembling hands. "You look, no, you are simply the most gorgeous goddess I have ever laid eyes on," he said. Yeah, I swooned just a bit. How could I not?

The whole hall was quiet, like the crowd was collectively holding its breath, waiting for something, anything, to happen. Apollo leaned forward and softly brushed his lips to my forehead and held them there for a moment or three. Every breath I had left my chest, and I felt dizzy, dazzlingly dizzy. But I regained my composure quickly. Tonight was not about dizziness or fluttery stomachs. It was about saving myself from a life of tortuous boredom and banality.

"As god of the heavens, I decree today a day of celebration, for tomorrow Thalia and Apollo will be married." It was my father, bellowing and bouncing me back to reality. The crowd roared with cheers. Daddy said a few more words about how overjoyed he was at this union, how "upstanding" and "noble" Apollo was, blah, blah, blah. When he finished, the crowd roared again, and all eyes were upon us.

Then the music began. Before I could even look at Polly or Era, Apollo had whisked me out onto the floor and was twirling me silly. Round and round, faster and faster. I relaxed a little. Apollo and I were together again, just being reckless kids as usual. I half forgot why everyone else was here as we spun from corner to corner. We were unstoppable.

We went round and round and round, and after a few minutes Apollo spotted icky King Cepheus.* Why on earth would Father have invited him? Apollo danced me right over there and twirled me just to ol' Cepheus's left, and oops, I stuck my foot out a hair too far, and down the big king went.

As we danced dance after dance, I couldn't deny it— I was having the time of my life with my best friend, who was not only silly and fun and smart but so very handsome, too. We talked; we joked; we teased each other mercilessly. I couldn't stop laughing—it was uncontrollable, coming up from my belly and taking over my whole body. I can enjoy this, I can enjoy him, I thought, without giving up any of myself, without actually marrying him. We danced and danced. We danced like wild children in our fancy clothes. We danced like Nereids dance in the deep blue sea. We danced like we were in love.

Then Hera had to speak and ruin the moment. "Excuse me, excuse me, everyone, for I have something to say."

"Doesn't she always," said the very charming Apollo.

---

* Remember him? The one who sacrificed his daughter? Ew.

"Ahem." Hera coughed, looking our way. "This is truly the happiest day of my life. To see this young and ill-tempered girl find some happiness just makes me want to cry." And then she made an attempt to eke out a tear, but to no avail.

"I just want to say that Apollo is the bravest of men for taming this wild child, for whom I have no more patience. And to him I am forever indebted. For her happiness, of course, not mine. Ahem."

"Dear, that's probably good enough," my father was cutting in, trying to spare the inevitable family embarrassment that comes whenever Hera speaks in public.

"No, no, I am not done quite yet. See, here come the tears. Tears of joy. With Thalia gone and off with her poor sap of a husband, oh, I mean savior of a husband, um, I will be entertaining every Friday night in my new music room, formerly Thalia's bedroom. Come on by if you'd like, and sing a tune or three with us."

At that, my father yanked Hera off the stage. A few of the guests fidgeted uncomfortably, but Hera's words didn't upset me in the least. I'd known since I was nine that Hera wanted me gone and out of the house. Ever since I'd playfully dyed her beloved cat, Manto, a lovely shade of violet.

What was upsetting was how my feelings for Apollo were taking over my brain. As he pulled me back onto the dance floor, his smile was exciting and made me feel warm from my toes to the ends of my hair. His eyes were like velvet; they welcomed me cozily into his arms. And his arms, oh, his arms, which were wrapped around me as we danced, felt gentle and yet so firm. My brain was just on fire. Could I have made the wrong decision in thwarting this whole marriage thing? I didn't know what to do. The time was approaching when I planned to make the Scyllia switch. I needed to find Polly and Era and talk to them about these flutters in my stomach and the ache in my chest. I needed to confess. I needed Polly's levelheadedness and Era's warmth to set me straight. I needed my two favorite sisters desperately.

Dingdong.

That was the bell announcing that the banquet was soon to begin. I had to find Polly and Era immediately. But before I could go more than a few steps, Apollo, with a sly smile, grabbed me by the arm and pulled me behind the giant curtain to the side of the stage.

He didn't say a word. He just took my face in his trembling hands. First his fingertips, soft, so soft, brushed over my lips. He held two perfectly straight fingers there for a moment and stared directly into my eyes. They were wet, actually wet, not with tears, just joy. And then his lips brushed mine, and he gently, ever so gently, kissed me. He tasted like blueberries. My throat went dry. My knees went weak. My fingertips tingled. My lower lip fluttered. And my eyes welled up.

When he pulled away, I just stared at him, dumb-founded. I couldn't speak. With his face just an inch or two from mine, he smiled his familiar devilish grin and then grabbed my waist, pulling me back onto the dance floor for a last go-round before supper.

I was in a serious state of confusion. Why had I fought this all along? I could not recall one reason, not one reason at all why I had not agreed to marry Apollo. Yet I knew I must have had reasons. I searched my brain, begging for an answer, a reason not to marry him. But nothing came. What a fool I had been. This marriage thing will be fine, I thought, grand, even. After all, he's the most beautiful kisser in the world and he tastes like ripe perfect fruit, not to mention he is brave, smart, crazy, wacky, and hilariously funny. And he loves me. He thinks I'm stunning. Inside and out.

Apollo took my hand and led me to the head table on the stage. He and I sat in the center. Hera sat to Apollo's right and Daddy to my left.

As everyone else took their seats, Hera leaned over to Apollo and me and said, "This has been all fun and games today, but after tomorrow you two will not behave as such children. You, Apollo, must tame her, for this behavior of tripping kings and insulting gods is unacceptable for a lady. As of tomorrow, it is done."

I then looked to Apollo to give me a roll of his eyes or to stick his finger down his throat to signal how horrendously gaggy that statement was, but instead he just said, "Yes, Your Highness. Of course."

And then he looked at me. His eyes were sorrowful, as if to say, "She's right; I'm sorry."

But she wasn't right. Since when did growing up mean not having fun? I looked at Apollo, who was now sitting upright, his manners perfectly in place. I looked at Hera with her smug satisfied smile, and then I looked back at Apollo. And like the flood that comes when Poseidon opens the dam on the river . . . it all came back to me. I remembered exactly why I didn't want to marry Apollo. Marry at all.

I had but moments to make a life-altering choice. I couldn't see straight. It seemed like the room was getting louder and louder. My eyes welled up out of pure confusion and fear. I looked for my sisters, and there they were, sitting at the opposite end of the table. Polly gave me an almost imperceptible nod.

The sound of tinkling crystal startled me. Daddy was raising his glass to make a toast, and all eyes were on me and Apollo. It was time to go through with this. I took a deep breath and held it there, just for a moment.

Then I took Hera's charmeuse bag out of my pocket and placed the hair of the goat boy inside. My two sisters' powers were already contained in the silky pink bag. I hooked my pinkie fingers together, closed my eyes, and envisioned toads and eels and sea monsters.

When I opened my eyes again, the first thing I focused on was the Furies, sitting a few seats away. They were huddled together, watching me, leaning forward and perfectly silent (which is pretty unusual for the Furies). And they were all wearing the same amused smiles. My skin swam with chills. Something was very, very wrong. But it was too late to do anything; the transformation had begun.

At first no one noticed. But then a huge green wart bubbled to the surface of my cheek and sprang a leak. It dripped neon green ooze from its tip. Apollo, Daddy, and the rest of the party all noticed at the same time. The crowd shrieked in horror, jumping out of their seats and knocking over place settings, chairs, tables.

I felt lost; the room was spinning out of control. My skin was changing second to second, and I couldn't focus on anyone or anything. I felt dizzy and sick. Really, genuinely, awfully sick.

Apollo's face was full of shock and concern. He went to grab my hand, but before he could touch me, Hera dove across him and at me, screaming, "Noooo, my music roooommmmmmm!" She clutched my shoulders and started shaking me furiously.

Then, not seconds later, her face began to simmer and boil with green ooze. Was I imagining it? Why would she have the dreaded Scyllia disease, too? But there she was, slime pouring out of her blooming sores in buckets, *her mouth wide open in one hideous, continuous scream. I couldn't help it—I started screaming, too.*

The hall was in complete pandemonium. For several minutes I gaped at the scene around me in confusion and horror. I clutched my own mouth to hold back my scream and found that my lips were covered in boils. I looked at Hera and saw my mirror image— her skin was a liquid green goo; her hair was now a pile of hissing snakes.

"Thalia!" Apollo cried, rushing toward me again. But one of the snakes now coiled on my own head hissed, and he backed off. The one and only thing Apollo is scared of is snakes. Era and Polly had also tried to rush to my side, but now they stood equally far away.

The hall was booming with gasps and screams and chatter. Several women had fainted.

"Please, everyone, keep quiet, stay calm," yelled Daddy, staring at Hera fearfully out of the corner of his eye and backing away just a bit farther.

When the transformation was finally complete and the ooze had slowed to a dribble, Hera's screams subsided to a dull moan, and she just stood there looking at me like she was going to tear me apart with her bare hands. But she couldn't get close enough because my serpent hair wanted a piece of hers, and bad. The snakes were coiled and hissing and ready to attack. The noises around us finally subsided to an expectant hush.

"What is the meaning of this?" Hera roared, indicating

her entire body, which was now mutated beyond recognition. Her voice echoed against the marble walls.

Then the Furies appeared at her side. They were the only ones who would, who could, go near her. The snakes were charmed by their presence and stopped their hissing.

"Oh, Hera, how we hate to be the bearers of bad news, but sweet queen, it was Thalia, Era, and Polly who concocted this scheme," said Meg, her voice dripping with happiness.

The crowd let out a collective gasp. I looked around, shocked and speechless. What could I say? It was true. I had never intended to give this horrible disease to Hera, but it was completely and thoroughly my fault. Although I had no idea how the Furies knew that.

Tizzie continued. "Thalia did not want to marry Apollo and thought of no other way than to—than to—give you the dreaded Scyllia disease. . . ."

"Wait a minute. That's not exactly right. No, no, no," I said.

But Alek picked up where Tizzie had stopped. "She thought that if they gave you the incurable Scyllia, it would cause a commotion and further prolong, if not halt, the wedding. Yes, that's it!"

"No, that's not it!" cried Era.

"It's not nearly that bad," cried Polly.

"And it's not incurable—I know how to reverse it

because . . ." I pleaded, looking at Daddy hopefully.

But Daddy did not let me finish. He let out a yell so loud, the huge, sparkling chandelier above us started to rock back and forth. And then it fell. The ground beneath us shook and crashed and crumbled as the chandelier shattered on the floor. I'm sure they felt that one on earth, I had time to think.

"Daddy." I struggled to hold back a flood of tears. "I—"

Just then I heard a sort of moan behind me. I turned to see Apollo standing there, looking more hurt than I had ever seen a man, animal, or god ever look. His eyes, so full of confusion, were no longer a sparkling green but a deep, dark, angry black. His lips were no longer round and ripe and red but tight and white and mad. His eyes caught mine, my now one lone green eye, and he said, "You gave this horrible disease to yourself to avoid marrying me?"

I opened my mouth, but no words would come out.

"In all our years as friends, I have never once lied to you. Never." He shuddered and shook his head. The look on his face sent stabbing pains of sorrow and shame through my heart.

"I—I . . ." I stammered, but he didn't let me finish. His expression turned from one of shock and pain into one of pure hatred, and he strode out of the hall.

"Daddy, please listen," Polly pleaded with him. "It wasn't our plan to hurt Hera. We—"

"Do you mean to tell me that you took part in this?" he bellowed. Polly looked down at the floor as if she wanted to sink right into it. And Era just started to cry silently. "I'm so utterly disappointed in you, Polly. I expect better from you. And you, Era . . ." He paused, shaking his head. "To your rooms, all three of you. Be gone. I cannot bear to look at your faces. Especially yours, Thalia—how could you do this to yourself? What in heavens were you thinking? Be gone!"

And with that the three of us sheepishly began our long walk out of the hall. The straggling guests were whispering and staring. I wanted to get out of that room as fast as I could. But I was especially slow. I had to drag around the thirty or forty serpents in my hair and an uncontrollable third arm that unfortunately kept pinching people's behinds as I walked by.

And the rest, as you know, is history. Ancient history, literally, but all too fresh in my mind. We went to bed that night, but none of us slept a wink before we were summoned to the throne room the next morning for our punishment.

NINETEEN

The Monday after the Tim disaster, it took a lot of convincing, but I got Polly and Era to come to the Grit for open-mike night. Yeah, we were the laughing-stock of the school and yeah, everyone we despised on this earth would be there, but I'd decided we needed to face our fears. We were stuck in this place for Zeus only knew how long, and I figured we needed to make the most of it.

Polly, of course, resisted. "Thalia, you must be out of your mind. There is no way I am ever setting foot anywhere near the Grit or high school or Tim Rhys ever again."

"Okay, I hear you. But look. Number one, there is no way we are going to do what Daddy wants us to do if we lock ourselves up in this house and cry about all the bad things that have happened. And number two, and more important, I think it's pretty darn important that we show people like the Backroom Betties and Tim that they can't keep us down. I refuse to stand for that. And I don't think you should, either." Polly shrugged halfheartedly.

"Look," I continued. "We are stuck here, and that is that. And I am not going to let this time on earth be a complete disaster. Until we get to go home, I'm going to have a life here, no matter what I have to do to get it. Come on, let's go. . . ." I pulled Polly up by the wrists. "That's all the inspirational speech I have in me today."

Era, who was easier to persuade, helped me drag Polly on the long walk down to the Grit.

As we walked in, most every eye was turned our way. Immediately we saw Tim, who was surrounded by the Backroom Betties, each one hanging on his every word. He looked our way with this annoying mixture of contempt and amusement. The Backroom Betties looked toward us, too, but *they* looked a little surprised to see us. Almost as if they'd thought we'd disappear off the face of the earth or something.

Polly hadn't regained one ounce of her confidence from my numerous pep talks. She stood there, on the verge of tears, unable to make eye contact with anyone. She shivered a little, shook a bit, and stared at the floor.

We took a small table off to the left of the stage.

Pocky came over and grabbed a chair, climbing on it backward. "Dude, I'm so sorry about what happened Friday; that, like, busts some nuts. That's, like, so raw. So uncool. That guy's an ape."

"That's very sweet; thank you, Pocky," said Polly. "You've been a good friend." I cocked an eyebrow Polly's way.

"Hey, no problem. If you want, I could sing you a little number up there, 'specially for you," Pocky offered.

"No!" said the three of us in unison. Visions of tigers of Bengali danced in my head. Polly said, "But thank you. You're awesome."

Pocky blushed.

Tim was up next, and the Backroom Betties all sat at a table right next to ours as he took the stage.

Tim walked up to the mike and thanked people, even though no one was clapping. He then said, "This is a little number I wrote a couple of months ago when I was going through some seriously messed-up stuff." He took a deep, dramatic breath and then counted off, "One and a two and a . . ."

He had a nice enough voice. I was kind of shocked. And the song, what I'd heard so far, was actually pretty good. It started out with stuff about leaving home, leaving your whole world behind. I was surprised at how thoughtful it was.

Polly clutched my arm, her nails digging into my

flesh. "Oh my God! That's the song I wrote. Oh, oh, oh," she cried. She was so stunned, she was virtually speechless. Her knees rattled, her shoulders shivered and hunched, she looked powerless and pitiful, and it angered me to my core.

I couldn't stand it—I had to do something. Who did this guy think he was?

If I used just a little bit of magic, Daddy and Hera probably wouldn't even find out. And even if they did, I was only using the teeniest bit. I only felt a moment's indecision. With a tiny twinkle of my nose I simply removed all traces of Polly from Tim's memory. This, of course, obliterated any memory of the song *Polly* wrote.

Tim's voice cracked. He grasped for the words; he coughed and strained and searched his brain.

Polly looked my way, one eyebrow cocked. Era giggled. People started to murmur.

But then all of a sudden, Tim's voice started ringing out loud and clear again. His face broke into a wide grin. He began to remember certain words and a partial tune. I must have screwed up. Hmpf.

But something was weird. I knew I'd used my powers correctly. And it wasn't just that. There was this weird feeling in the air. I couldn't really figure out what it was, but it made my stomach turn and my heart flip-flop. It was this feeling of something bad all around me. A feeling I had only felt a rare few times, back on Olympus when . . .

I shook my head to clear it. I was obviously just rusty, following in my father's footsteps, no doubt. I twinkled my nose again, exasperated. And Tim went blank again. He stood up there like a lost child. His mouth just making gibberish noises. *There*.

But then he bounced back. A little. He sang a few more words, strummed a few more chords. I wrinkled my nose, and again he stopped singing.

Stray bits of laughter issued from the crowd. For a moment I couldn't help smiling—it would serve Tim right to be laughed at by everyone he knew. But then something, some kind of intuition, made me look to my left.

That's when I noticed that three people were definitely not laughing. Three girls who obviously did not think this was funny at all. Three girls who were staring directly at me.

I locked eyes with Teri, the queen of the Backroom Betties, and tried to hold her stare. She returned my gaze—with eyes as dark and depthless as Hades itself. And then her bloodred lips parted into the whitest, evilest of all evil smiles. I *knew* that smile. And I knew that feeling of evil that surrounded this entire room. It was the feeling of someone using their powers for no good. In a blinding flash everything clicked into place: the Backroom Betties' rude notes, their arrival at school just a few weeks ago, their sudden friendship with Tim. . . .

And suddenly I knew. Those girls might not look the same, but it was clear—I was playing tug-of-war for Tim's memory with the indomitable, the merciless, the incomparably evil . . . Furies!

The three girls all turned their attention back toward the stage. Did they know that I knew? And why were they here? I grabbed Polly's arm, but she was mesmerized by what was going on onstage. She looked like she actually felt bad for Tim. I tugged at both of my sisters' arms until they turned to look at me.

"Watch this," I whispered. I twinkled my nose, and Tim's memory was gone. Moments later the black-haired Betty to our right wiggled her right eyebrow, and Tim's memory returned, albeit crudely. I twinkled, they wiggled, I twinkled, they wiggled until Tim sounded like a warbling lorikeet. People gasped and laughed and pointed.

"I don't get it," said Era.

"What's going on?" asked Polly, extremely suspiciously.

"Look over *there,*" I said, nodding toward the table next to us, and twinkled again. And so did the Betty. And Tim choked and crackled.

Era's eyes became huge, round saucers. She sucked in her bottom lip and bit it with her teeth. Polly just turned white. "It can't be. No, no, really?" she said. Her face was a mask of shock. "How? Why?" But then she glanced toward the stage, and that fear turned to anger in two seconds flat. "What are they doing to Tim?!" she cried, jumping out of her chair. Well, that wasn't the reaction I was expecting.

"Giggle butt, do dew hut, la," sang Tim. His friend who had been spinning behind him just stood staring, his mouth hanging wide open.

My sister looked flushed and excitable as she jumped up onto the stage and grabbed Tim. She held on to his shoulder and whispered soothingly in his ear. I, meanwhile, had stopped my twinkling to watch this bizarre spectacle unfold. Polly stood beside the babbling Tim and began to sing. Slowly, sweetly, calmly. It had been ages since I'd heard Polly's sweet and mesmerizing voice solo.

I glanced over at the Furies, who sat stock-still, watching Polly.

With my sister singing, the song Tim had been singing was much moodier. Haunting, almost. The DJ, snapping out of his daze, spun a jazz beat behind her, and she let out a coo that seemed to melt the heart of every boy and girl in the place. The crowd, after whispering and tittering for the first minute or two, fell silent. They were as enchanted with Polly as Era and I were. And this was no spell. Tim, who had just been standing there looking dumbfounded, started to come to.

Polly closed her eyes and put everything she had into that song. It was fantastic, no, beyond fantastic, explosive. And I'm not just saying that because she's my sister. It left me covered in goosebumps.

As the song ended, the crowd actually jumped to their feet and started cheering. Guys were hooting in the back. Tim turned to Polly, now fully recovered, and just let out a guttural, "Whoa."

She smiled, patted him on the back, and walked off the stage confidently. People ran up to her and told her how beautiful her voice was and how awesome she sounded. They were clamoring to talk to her. The only people who weren't cheering were the Furies, of course. They were just sitting there, scowling.

Then Teri got up and walked over to our table. She stood above us, glowering.

I stood up to face her. "We know who you are. I don't know how you got here or what you're doing here, but whatever it is, let me tell you, we are not the least bit scared of you. Not the least." I looked down at Era for backup, and she nodded loyally.

Teri just smiled, but I could tell underneath it all, she was boiling with anger. "My dear Thalia, if you aren't scared of us yet, you should be." Her grin widened.

With that, Teri walked back to the other two girls, and the three of them made their way through the crowd and out of the café. And even though they kept their noses in the air as they walked out, I could tell they felt defeated.

I watched the Furies go, feeling relief wash over me. They were gone, at least for now. And Polly was standing in the middle of a crowd of admirers, beaming, despite what were obviously the Furies' best efforts to crush her spirit.

My superstar sister walked back to our table, with Pocky following behind her like a puppy. When she stopped, he dropped to his knees in front of her and said, "You are a true goddess. I worship at your tiny feet of love."

Polly looked down at him, looked over at me, flashed me her very biggest grin, and said, "Get up, Pocky."

TWENTY

"Do you girls need a lift?"

It was Pocky, outside the club.

"No thanks," said Polly. "Although that's very sweet. I think I could just float home, I am so blissfully happy. I think we'll walk. Is that all right, girls?"

"Fine by me," said Era.

"Me too," I said.

The last hour or so had been simply fabulous. Era and I had sat back and watched the crowds swarm our sister with praise and adulation. She had her confidence back; she was feeling independent and beautiful.

"You know that guy named Guy?" she asked. "He asked me to be in his band. Isn't that a hoot?"

"That's more than a hoot—that's a holler. You're too good for him!" I said.

"Oh, stop, Thalia. I said I would think about it. He likes all that feedback stuff, which really isn't my thing, but maybe I will give it a try. Jo-Jo, the DJ, he said he'd play with me again in a heartbeat."

"Of course he would. You killed 'em."

"It really was so much fun," she gushed.

"Yeah, except for the part where we discovered the Furies are here on earth and plan to make our lives miserable," I replied.

Polly's face fell. "Oh. You know, it's funny. I kind of forgot about that."

"You know they're going to hurt our chances of getting home. They're going to do everything in their immense power to stop us from succeeding," I said soberly.

"They almost already did. I mean, I was so ready to give up on everything just a few hours ago," Polly said.

"Yeah, but now that we know who they are, we know what we're fighting, right?" Era said hopefully. "And besides, did you see how they slunk out of the club after you were done singing? Ha! You *so* showed them," added Era.

"But don't think for a second that they aren't going to enact a little revenge our way. They're all about the tit for a tat—they can match us, step for step," said Polly.

"You know what?" I said. "Good."

"Good?" my sisters asked in unison.

"Yeah, good! They might make this place a little more exciting."

"I think it's plenty exciting," said Polly, the hint of a smile playing at her lips.

"No, we need a little fiery competition thrown in the mix. We need a little adventure. And face it, the Furies can supply that, tenfold."

"It might mean not getting home as quickly, though," said Era.

I looked at Polly, who looked at Era, who then looked back at me. Then we looked back toward the Grit, where people were still laughing and talking and buzzing. And each of our faces broke out into a giant, goofy grin.

✳ ✳ ✳

So they think they beat us, well, maybe this once,
But we've got some plots and even more stunts
That will send the Muses' heads a-spinning.
Oh, take our word, this is just the beginning.
They're happy now, but the Muses will see
That earth life is not all it's cracked up to be.
Polly will fall, and Era will fail—
We'll make sure they're sent to a fiery jail.
Most sadly of all, once they get to that den,

Dear Thalia will never see Apollo again.
But to find out the rest, why, that is the hook:
The next tale unfolds in a whole 'nother book!

❋ ❋ ❋

And until then, good night.

IF YOU THOUGHT THIS
BOOK WAS GOOD, TAKE
A SNEAK PEEK AT
GODDESSES 2,
THREE GIRLS AND A GOD

PROLOGUE

Our story finds our three Greek goddesses in a land unfamiliar—earth. Athens, Georgia, 2002, to be exact. Forced by their father, the great Zeus, and their evil stepmother, Hera, to go to high school, get good grades, and use none of their goddess powers, they must each complete a special challenge to return to their heavenly home. And while they know the Furies are in town to torture and torment and keep them from reaching their goals, they have, thus far, foiled the evil ones' evil plans. Still, the girls are wary, for it's almost certain that the Furies are, at this very moment, planning their demise.

Meanwhile in Olympus, Apollo, heartbroken and distraught, is clueless as to the real whereabouts of his spunky true love. . . .

ONE

Throp.

"Ungh."

Throp.

"Grunt."

Throp. Bounce. Bounce. Bounce.

"Ow! Hey, sir, I thought you said we were square," cried Apollo, who had just been grazed on the ear by a lightning-fast tennis ball.

"I win again," exulted Zeus with a grin, revealing a set of teeth as bright as the moon.

"Yes, again. You win *again*. Is this making you feel better? Because it's not really helping me." Apollo rubbed his ear, scowling. That ball had hurt.

"Why, yes, I do believe it is making me feel a tad better," Zeus answered cheerfully. "Thank you. Anyway, it's just good to get out of the house. It's been a touch depressing with those three girls gone. Thalia was always making me laugh, and I miss Polly's seriousness, her beautiful stoicism. And, well, Era, I miss the frivolity she brought to the palace. You know," Zeus continued, tugging at his beard, "I have been meaning to ask you—how are you doing, young man? Have my daughter's reckless shenanigans gotten the better of you?"

But Zeus didn't really want to know, and he didn't bother waiting for the answer. He just continued. "She's a handful, that one." He let out a long sigh. "Thalia, oh, Thalia. As much as I would have liked to have seen a match between you two, and, well, Hera would have loved it . . . er, Hera." With these words Zeus paused, cringing a little. "You know she still has some lingering green around the ears, but she is a bit consoled by the addition of that music room out of Thalia's old bedroom. Although I told her, I don't know how long Thalia will be gone, but she—"

"Sir, with all due respect, this is the very matter I want to speak to you about. This tennis game was just a ruse."

"Is that so?" said Zeus with a leering eye. He wasn't paying all that much attention to Apollo. He was concentrating on a tiny little lint ball that he'd just noticed on his shoulder. He just wasn't able to grab it.

"Well, yes, you see, I've thought long and hard," said Apollo, "and I haven't slept for a month at least, not since the party, the incident, the Scyllia, and the green ooze. Not since Thalia was sent away."

"That explains the lousy tennis game. I may be Zeus, but you are considerably younger than I. Beating you was a bit too easy."

"Um, yes, perhaps. Anyway, I want to speak with you about Thalia," said Apollo.

Zeus looked a little exasperated. "What do you want? I owe you for sure—just name it. Jewels? A higher title? A different daughter? What?"

"No, I don't want a payoff, no, sir." Apollo was a little insulted by the implication, but he carried on. "I do want something, though. I want . . . Thalia."

Zeus's eyes widened. "Are you mad? After what she did to you, to me, to Hera? Thalia will be lucky if any man wants to marry her at this rate. She might as well truly be green for all the men she'll attract."

"Please don't talk about her like that," demanded Apollo. Zeus's eyes revealed he didn't like being spoken to as such, so Apollo followed up with, "I say that respectfully, of course."

Apollo then began to walk and talk. "I've thought about this a lot. All those sleepless hours and, see, maybe Thalia isn't ready for marriage just yet, today or tomorrow. I now know it was foolish of me to rush into things without openly communicating my feelings to her. She was blindsided. I don't blame her for the way she acted."

"I know someone who does," Zeus said out of the side of his mouth as he conjured up a picture of his oozing, pussing, chartreuse wife.

Apollo was getting more nervous by the second. His hands were trembling; his voice even cracked. But he knew he had to defend Thalia. He knew others didn't understand her, not even her own father, but that didn't matter. He just wanted Thalia to come back home. "Well, *I* don't blame her, sir. And I think we just need a chance to talk, Thalia and I, and we can work this out. I think I would like very much for Thalia to be my—my—my—well, if she will have me, my girlfriend. And see, I think, no, I know, deep down in the pit of my stomach, I know Thalia has great, wondrous feelings for me."

Apollo twitched a little. He rubbed his nose. And then he said, more quietly, more thoughtfully, with a small smile, "Your daughter is the most special, incredible, creative, dangerous girl I have ever known. Your daughter is everything to me." He couldn't stop wringing his hands, rubbing them together, faster and faster. He gulped for air and then said, "I have come here to ask you to return her, and her sisters, of course, to Olympus."

Now the whole time Apollo had been making this speech, he paced. As he paced, so did Zeus, just two steps behind. The two men slowly switched feet back and forth. They weren't on a tennis court, in the traditional sense. It was more like a flat mountaintop on the peak of a very tall summit. And now they were moving around it freely. And while Apollo wasn't paying much attention to where he stepped, Zeus was. Right at the end of the speech Apollo went a step too far and almost went feet first down the mountainside. Zeus nabbed him by the back of his white robe and brought his feet back down to the dirt. Apollo didn't even notice. He was lost in his thoughts of Thalia.

Zeus did seem a bit touched by the young god's sentiment. He softened his shoulders. A small smile crept over his bearded face. He felt admiration for Apollo, who so obviously loved his wild-at-heart daughter. But then he said quite plainly, rather simply, "No."

"Of course you can, c'mon," said Apollo, who thought perhaps Zeus was just playing with him. Making him beg.

"No, I really can't. I don't believe they have learned their lessons just yet."

"They can learn their lessons here in Olympus. This is unreasonable. Please, Zeus, for me?" Now Apollo was really begging.

"Look, Apollo, the girls, they hurt more than just you. Have you taken a look, a long look, at my wife lately? Why, I daresay I've never, ever seen her this angry, this incredulous, this abominably hate-filled in all my days. And I have a lot of days, if you know what I mean." Zeus was trying to be conversational, chummy, almost, with Apollo. But it just made Apollo more frustrated.

"That's what this is really about, isn't it? Hera has her grips in you. These are your daughters, your flesh and blood. How can you do this to them?"

"Apollo, this may be what Hera mandates, yes, but make no mistake, I believe this to be in their best interest. They need time away from the vast comforts of home." In one sweeping gesture Zeus took in their surroundings. "Look around, Apollo—we live in heaven. Literally! Life here is easy. The girls were free to do as they pleased here, and they took great liberties with that freedom. Planning such a hoax, spoiling a perfectly good party, turning their stepmother green! Thalia is selfish. And the other two, well, they are practically grown, yet look at their behavior!" Zeus's face had grown quite red by this point. "One can't make a decision without the other; they meddle in business that is not their own. I love them all, but those girls have proved themselves to be spoiled and ungrateful. You of all people should understand that!"

Apollo's forehead wrinkled. His eyes darkened a shade or two. "Well, I do not. I don't understand. I don't understand how a father can banish his girls to foreign soil, with no care or worry for their happiness. With no one to watch over them!"

"Oh, well . . ." Zeus stumbled a bit over his words here. "Hermes will be taking notes to the girls from time to time, I assure you. . . . And, er, you see, Hera has sent a few to look over them," he continued, looking like he would be keen to change the subject.

"Who? Who, then?"

"This was not my territory," Zeus said quietly, almost in a whisper. He actually looked ashamed. His crazy eyebrows turned downward, and his face scrunched a bit to show his wrinkles. "She sent the Furies."

Apollo stood there, wide-eyed in disbelief. Then he screamed, "The *who*?"

"You heard me"—and this last part he really did whisper—"the Furies. They're posing as three mortal girls down on earth, at Thalia's high school."

"Oh, blast me! Oh, what have you done? What were you thinking?"

"They might not have been the best choice for the job, but frankly, the decision was not mine to make. Hera took care of it right after I banished the girls."

"That's just great. Just plum. No, that's it—now I demand you return the girls, or I will just have to go retrieve them myself!" Apollo's own handsome face was tweaked unrecognizably from anger. He was frantic at this point.

Zeus held back his laughter. He actually got a kick out of young insubordinates like Apollo. And Thalia. But he knew this was serious.

"You forget who I am. I am the great and powerful Zeus!" And with that, lightning filled the whole sky. It happened every time he uttered those seven words. It was one of his favorite tricks.

Apollo crumpled to the ground and sat there in a lifeless heap. He was worn out, tired, exhausted with worry and fear and love. He gasped for energy, for breath, for words. "Please, Zeus, you are indeed powerful, great, even, I daresay, mighty. Please let me go and bring back Thalia."

Zeus looked slightly amused. Apollo wondered if it could be that he was responding to the flattery. Apollo thought it best to make the most of it. "You are in fact the single most powerful being in the whole of the universe, and you command respect from all corners of the universe." Apollo was clinging to the flattery as if it were his last hope of bringing back Thalia. "Your stature, it is envied by everyone, every single being, both animal and human. Your strength is unparalleled, your wisdom unmatched. And did I mention attractive? You are a stunning-looking fellow and—"

"Okay, enough. This is getting pathetic, really. I

don't need some kid telling me how handsome and strong I am. But I do like you. I tell you what. I will make you a deal."

Apollo's eyes perked up. His ears twitched. He jumped to his feet with renewed energy.

"You may go down to earth. But I cannot let you go as yourself, for Hera specifically forbids 'Apollo's' earthly assistance. Therefore you must go as someone else. You must go in disguise."

"Sure, a disguise. Maybe a goat or an old cobbler."

"Now, listen, you may not retrieve the girls. However, you may help them along in their efforts to fulfill the challenges Hera and I have set in front of them. Once they complete those challenges, they are free to return home."

"Oh, thank you, Zeus. You won't regret this," said a smiling Apollo, who hadn't grinned like this since his and Thalia's engagement party. The one where she turned herself green to avoid marrying him (and, thanks to the Furies, accidentally turned Hera green in the process).

"But wait, this is delicate. You must listen and obey, or the girls' very lives are at stake. Remember, I forbid you to tell the girls who you are. If they find out, Hera will surely banish you to the nether reaches of Hades for all eternity, and I suspect my girls will never be allowed back in Olympus. Hera has the power. And as much as it pains me, I am fairly certain she wants them gone for good. Any misstep, any mistake, any reason to banish them forever, and I fear she will jump at the opportunity. The Furies have already reported some small use of magic, and it's taken a lot of cajoling on my part, and quite a lot of jewelry, to keep Hera from inflicting the strictest punishment. Do you understand the severity of the situation? Do you understand the dire consequences of your actions?"

Apollo understood. Down to his bare feet. His whole body shivered at the thought. "I've got it, sir. Thank you again for this opportunity."

"Please keep your goal close to your heart. Your purpose, Apollo, is to assist the girls with their earthly challenges. You may encourage Thalia to be more selfless, Era to be more assertive and strong, and Polly to find her own way, her own life—but nothing more. This is not the time to try to win my daughter's heart, do you understand?"

"Yes, of course. I will leave tonight."

"And make sure they're getting good grades in this school. Hera is chomping at the bit to see one of them fail."

"Yes, sir, of course."

After a quick bow Apollo turned on his heels. His heart was glowing, the hope inside him renewed. He headed toward the court exit.

But Zeus stopped him. "Apollo, there is one more thing." He took a deep, almost cavernous breath.

"You know my daughters were sent to earth. But what you don't know is, I accidentally banished the girls . . . into the future."

"Whoa," Apollo replied, stopping in midstep. "Okay." He really didn't know what to say to that.

"And," continued Zeus, "it appears I have sent them to the United States of America."

All Apollo could muster in response was a quiet, "Huh?"

Zeus closed his eyes, bowed his head, and sheepishly said, "You'll find the girls in Athens . . . Georgia, um, 2002."

Apollo blinked a few times, bowed again, and continued on his way. He'd have to figure out the details later—this was a lot to take in. He had no idea what this new place or time would be like. He didn't even know if they would have goats or cobblers there.

But then, maybe a goat or a cobbler wasn't quite the right disguise for this journey. Because even though Apollo planned to follow most of Zeus's rules, he couldn't help thinking that maybe, just maybe, he'd be able to win Thalia's heart a little while he was with her on earth. And to do that, he needed the right image.

So the big question was, what was he going to wear?